STRA… IN THE … PROMISED LAND

NOVELLA

JIM WILBOURNE

Published by Emergent Realms

https://www.emergentrealms.com/

Edited by Adryanna Monteiro

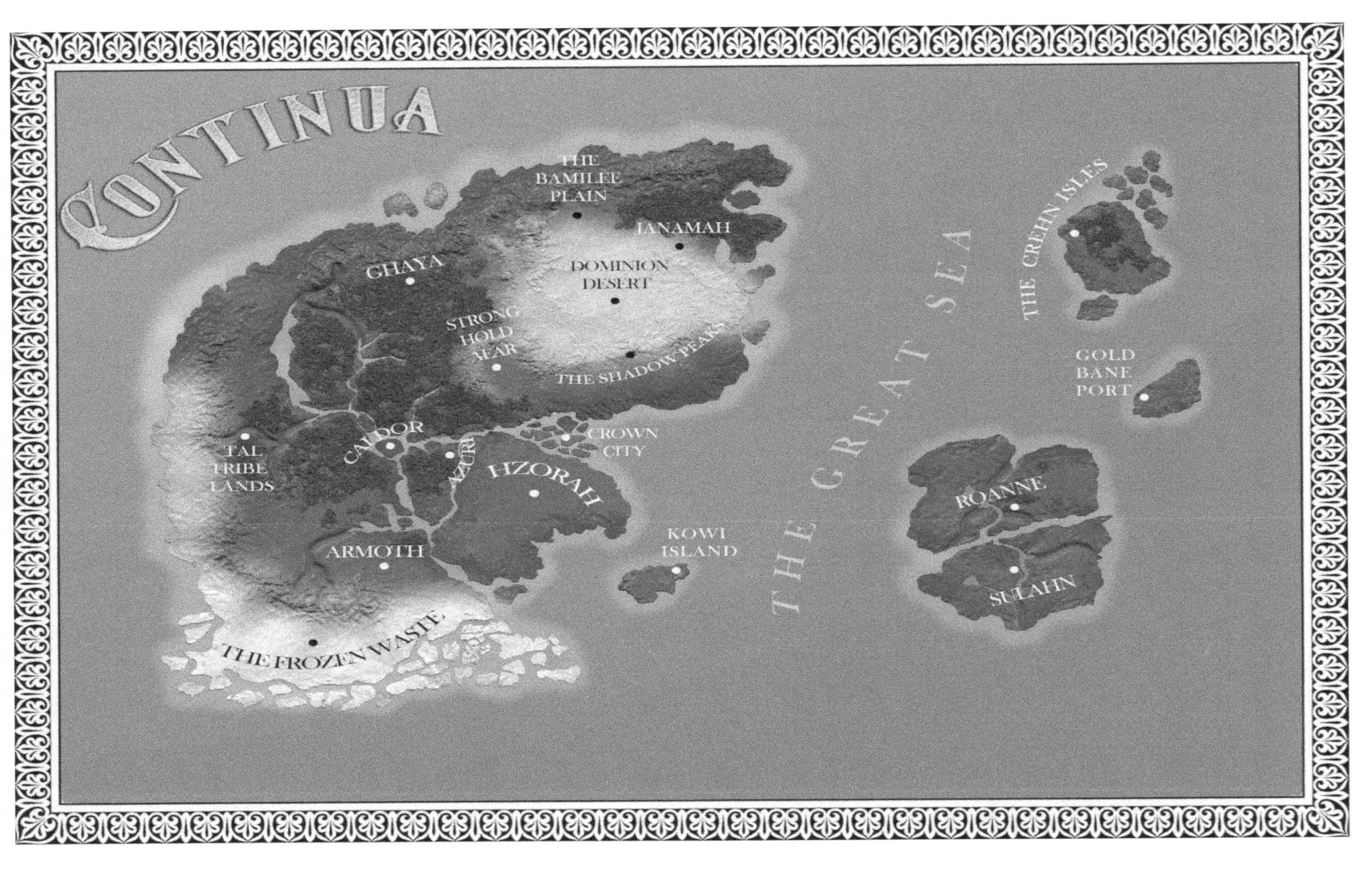
CONTINUA
THE BAMILEE PLAIN
JANAMAH
DOMINION DESERT
GHAYA
STRONG HOLD AFAR
THE SHADOW PEAKS
CALDOR
AZURI
CROWN CITY
TAL TRIBE LANDS
HZORAH
ARMOTH
KOWI ISLAND
THE FROZEN WASTE
THE GREAT SEA
THE CREHN ISLES
GOLD BANE PORT
ROANNE
SULAHN

ONE

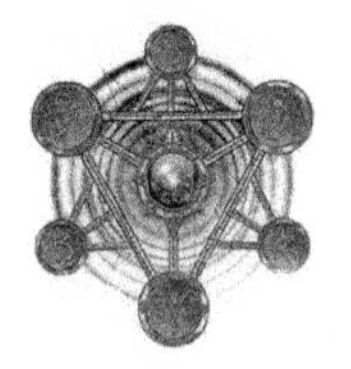

THE PROMISED LAND

There wasn't much to be said about the promised land. Rocks, trees, grass, birds, goats. Nothing Tarub hadn't seen before, and nothing he wouldn't see again. The austere and unassuming landscape affronted his sense of justice, crushed his anticipated catharsis. And for the first time in his short, self-assured nineteen years, Tarub found himself doubting.

He'd been born here, though he wasn't exactly sure where. The promised land was vast, and the vague notion of "further south" meant little to him in a place he couldn't remember. Eveletia was supposed to be a great city—beautiful beyond anything he'd ever seen—so there was little chance he'd miss his birthplace when he arrived. But he'd also been told that the promised land was an absolute vision. Perhaps, over the past decade, the old folk had an exaggerated memory of the place.

Of course, the vast wasteland that separated the city of Janamah and the fertile grounds of the Bamilee Plain from the northern reaches of the promised land exemplified a hellscape. After his ma and pa had wandered the desert seeking a new life—hoping that Titan's blessings would lead them from one safe harbor to another—Tarub imagined that a romanticized view of their homeland was normal if not expected. He'd traveled across the waste, and he'd avoid doing it again if he could.

And that was exactly their plan.

Tarub watched as Rossok and Normand made camp in the small clearing just off the narrow road. He wasn't completely unable to help, but Rossok had insisted that Tarub rest while he and Normand took care of preparations. Tarub had come out of the battle far worse off than the two of them, but it was still uncomfortable watching his friends work without him. The arrow wound hadn't been fatal, but it was certainly enough to keep him from exerting himself.

Pushing past the sharp pain in his shoulder, Tarub tugged at the tight collar of the Hzorah troops uniform before he reached for his pack and pulled it close. There was little for food inside, but perhaps that was Titan's justice for what they'd done—for the grave sin that brought them here.

And now, he doubted that too. Perhaps they shouldn't be here. Maybe they should go back and beg for their lives and a chance to rejoin the cause.

Rossok and Normand approached and squatted down beside him. "That should do it for firewood," Rossok said. "Are you enjoying being prince for the day?"

"For a day?" Tarub grunted. "I take an arrow for you and a day is all I get?"

Rossok smirked. "*For* me? You practically fell into it."

Tarub didn't think of himself as a soldier. His father was a brick mason, and Tarub had always assumed he'd follow in his father's footsteps. He wasn't like Rossok, who'd trained for years in the Creed's army. But he also wasn't at all like Normand, who would do better wielding a pen than a sword or spear.

"I know I make light of your injury," Rossok said,

placing a hand on his shoulder. "But I'm truly grateful to have a friend who'd take an arrow for me."

Rossok's experience in the Creed's army meant that he outranked Tarub and Normand. Tarub wasn't a poor fighter, but he was nothing next to Rossok. And that's why he'd taken that arrow for him. Not because he was a good friend, but because it was better that Tarub die than Rossok. It's what Titan would have wanted.

"Think nothing of it," Tarub said. He fell silent for a moment, his thoughts turning once again to his doubt. "Hardly seems worth it."

Rossok looked at him. "Hmm?"

Tarub nodded to the tree line. "All this. The promised land. I took an arrow to reclaim it. We lost thousands of men and maybe would have lost them all if it weren't for Titan's blessed intervention with those ice monsters."

"It's not about the land," Normand said. "Not entirely. It's about Titan's will—his longing to return to us and his desire to see the world remade. It's about what's right."

Normand had always been the spiritual one in their company of the Creed's army. And that made him all the more unusual for going along with Rossok's plan to desert. He'd looked horrified when Rossok suggested that they steal and don the uniforms of their enemy. Even now, he looked away, as if horrified that he'd found himself on the wrong side of history.

Tarub and Rossok knew their rites in spirit, but Normand had them memorized. In a different time—a more peaceful time—Normand would have been an invaluable asset to the clergy, serving the people's spiritual needs at the Shrine of the Creed. Instead, he'd found himself on the frontlines.

"Don't worry yourself," Rossok said. "It's over now. And that's more than the poor bastards who retreated with the army can say."

Normand rubbed his forehead. "What if they find out? What if the prophet sends soldiers after us? What—"

"After us?" A smile crossed Rossok's face. "You can't honestly believe that we're important enough for the prophet to drop everything and scoop us up. He let half his scorching army die against the Shadow Peaks! We're nothing to him."

Normand stared off into the distance. "We all have our place—"

"Oh, shove off!" Rossok growled. He stood and paced a half-circle before turning back. "Look. We're not going to get caught. You wanted to live in the promised land, right?" He raised his arms and took a deep breath. "Here we are. You didn't want to cross the wilderness again, and we're not. We're free."

"But will they accept us?" Tarub said. "That's still the part I'm worried about. They hate us here."

"We'll find a place to live that won't ask too many questions," Rossok said.

"What if we can't?" Normand asked.

"Then we kill them."

Normand's eyes went wide.

"I'm kidding!" Rossok settled back down beside Tarub. "We'll make this work. We can't go back now. It's too late for that. We don't have any other choice."

Somewhere in the back of Tarub's mind he'd known the truth of that. They crossed the point of no return by deserting. Sure, they could attempt to rejoin the army quietly and hope that no one noticed—that they'd gotten separated and only just found their way back—but Tarub didn't want that either.

"Our actions," Normand began, "are not without grave consequence. We may find a way to live in peace, but at what cost? We have made Titan's return harder still. Perhaps we have delayed his return by a small measure, but every action counts. 'For together we await, and together we must fulfill.'"

Tarub bowed his head as guilt washed over him. This was wrong. Maybe he should go back. He couldn't make it back on his own, but if Normand felt the same way, maybe they could get Rossok to repent too.

It's never too late to do the right thing. That's what Ma had always said. *There are consequences to doing the wrong thing, but there is no grace without recompense.*

Despite the fear of fighting another battle and hope of prosperity in the promised land, staying wasn't the right thing to do. "We should—" Tarub began but was cut off.

"Who's that?" Normand asked, standing.

Tarub looked up to see Normand pointing down the road near the clearing. Rossok stood, and Tarub turned as fast as his shoulder pain would allow.

"Should we hide?" Tarub asked.

"No," Rossok said. "No, we couldn't hide our camp fast enough. But I don't think two women will be much of a problem."

"What are they doing out here?" Normand asked.

"I don't know," Rossok said. "But they have a horse. We could use a horse."

Normand looked to Rossok. "We can't take their horse. That wouldn't be right."

"They're heathens," Rossok said, his jaw clenched.

"*We're* heathens," Tarub said. "We are now, at least."

Rossok looked to him. "We're not like them. We may have deserted, but we fought for Titan's return. That's more than anyone here can say."

"I still don't feel right about it," Normand said.

Rossok stared down the road with keen interest. "I don't think we have to."

TWO

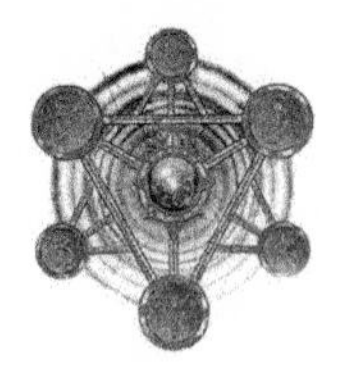

COMPANIONS

Mara grabbed hold of her sister's arm. "Stop."

Amie turned to her, a crease of worry etched on her face. "What is it? Do you need a rest?"

"No," Mara said. "Look ahead. Do you see that?"

Amie turned back to the path before them, and for what felt like an agonizingly long five seconds, Amie searched for what Mara thought was obvious.

"Smoke?" Amie whispered as she turned back to her older sister, her blue eyes wide with concern.

Mara nodded. "Smoke. There's someone there."

This was exactly what Mara worried would happen. After they had been captured by Dominion soldiers in their home in Azuri, Mara had watched her father die in a cramped, iron-barred cart, sat helpless as her sister, Amie, tried to weasel her way out of the grip of their brutish captors, and suffered an injury to the head that she suspected qualified as a concussion. And while they were in a much better position to survive now than they were as prisoners, they were lost, alone, and had little to nothing for supplies.

And now soldiers.

Perfect. Just perfect.

"Maybe we should turn back," Amie said, her hand absently resting on their horse's nose. "Maybe we can hide."

Mara shook her head. "No. The bend of the road has given them the visual advantage. They probably chose this spot specifically for this reason. If they're at all competent, they would have spotted us already. We're not equipped to run. That horse—"

"Saleh."

"—is injured and can't run. I'm relatively certain that I have a concussion and shouldn't over-exert myself. Hiding a horse isn't exactly something that can be done if they've already spotted us. They'll know to look for us and won't overlook us so easily, even if we do somehow find a way to camouflage him."

Amie turned back to look at the path. "So, what do we do?"

"Unfortunately," Mara sighed, "we should risk happening upon them. If we're lucky, they'll leave us alone. If we're unlucky, they'll be hostile."

"There's a third option," Amie whispered. "Maybe they'll help."

"I stand corrected. There are three ways this might go." Mara said as she squinted into the distance. A rush of relief washed over her. "I don't think this will be like last time. We're not being pulled out of our home, and those are Hzorah soldiers. They're on our side."

As they continued down the path, Mara continued to hold Amie's arm for support. She didn't enjoy having to depend on her sister to keep her upright, but it was entirely impractical to go on without help. If she was to get them back home, she had to be alive and well.

She'd had to take it slow since they'd left the Shadow Peaks two days ago. They'd taken frequent breaks, which Amie often said was for the horse's benefit. But Mara wasn't stupid, and she hated that it made her feel patronized.

Ever since their mother died, Father had told her that she, Mara, was responsible for the welfare of her sister. Of course, he didn't say it in so many words, but she knew that Father depended on her to be there for him, always, and to keep Amie out of trouble. She took that responsibility seriously.

Running the most prestigious tavern in West Hzorah's largest settlement that sat on Hzorah's most important trade route presented countless opportunities for cheats, thieves, and general misconduct after a long night of drinking. Her father had been a big man who could break up a fight and make someone think twice before risking a scheme, but Mara was the Kruv House's first line of defense.

And Amie . . . Well, Amie didn't tend to make her job easier. Between her general lack of interest in keeping a well-maintained inn to her tendency to get herself caught up in hijinks of other children her age, Mara had her hands full.

Mara's horrifying dread was never more complete when Amie had managed to get one of the Deseran soldiers who'd captured them to pull them out of the cart. She was certain that Amie would get them killed.

But she hadn't. *This* time.

And now, Father was gone. She and Amie were alone.

She couldn't depend on Father to help where Amie could not or would not. She couldn't go to him to ask him for advice, to have him calm her down when she'd absolutely had it with her sister, to—

A tear slipped down her cheek and settled on her chin. Before Amie noticed, she rubbed her face against the shoulder of her nightshift. She couldn't allow Amie to see her crying. One of them had to have their wits about them.

At least they'd finally run into someone who could help.

Amie's sister was many things—most of them admirable. Sentimental was not one that Amie would put on that list. And so, when Amie caught her sister wiping away a tear, she didn't ask her what was wrong. She didn't even look at her, as to not draw attention to the fact that she'd noticed. That would only provoke Mara's wrath.

Their time together on the road wasn't exactly a bard's tale. Her feet were still blistered, her legs ached, and despite the beautiful spring weather, the nights were cold enough that the one piece of clothing she had—a thin nightshift—was hardly adequate at keeping the night's chill from seeping into her bones.

She wanted good food, a bed, a warm hearth, and most of all: boots. Their journey thus far had been so horrible that it *almost* made her want to eagerly retire to a life of quiet anonymity at the Kruv House.

Almost.

But life as an innkeeper wasn't to be her future. They would have to return to Azuri and put their father's affairs in order first, but Mara had said that the future was in Caldor with Tele, Navid, and Gavini. Their future was more adventure. And that was . . . marvelous!

Amie had had more than a lifetime of adventure these past few months, for sure, but Caldor would certainly be a different kind of adventure. The kind she'd actually been wanting while chained to the Kruv House kitchens. She'd finally get to see a beautiful city, meet new and exotic people, and perhaps even fall in love with a handsome boy. More than anything, that's what kept her walking on cold, blistered feet.

But now, things might be looking up. If Amie's hopes about the people just ahead were true, they had a good chance at a more pleasant journey home. They could have food or a spare cloak or boots. *Oh please, let it be boots!*

As they neared the camp, a man trotted up to the path

and waved at them. He wore a dusty Hzorah soldier's uniform and a pleasant smile. Mara's grip tightened on her arm, and Amie slowed to a halt before giving Saleh a gentle pat on the nose.

"Easy," Amie whispered to him. "He looks nice enough."

"At least he's one of ours," Mara whispered. "Perhaps you were right."

Amie looked at her sister. "Was that a compliment? Are you feeling well?"

Mara frowned. "It wasn't a compliment. It was an acknowledgment."

"Right," Amie said, turning back to the soldier so Mara wouldn't see the smirk on her face.

"Are you girls lost?" the man asked with an easy smile.

"Lost?" Amie said. "No. Just taking a stroll in our underthings."

The man's smile widened, and he pointed to his two companions just off the path. "My friends and I are on the way home from war. If you'd like to join us, we have food."

Food. Amie's heart lurched with joy at the prospect of a good meal. She looked at her sister, checking if Mara was thinking what she was thinking, but Mara didn't catch her eye. Instead, her head was bowed, and she looked as if she might collapse. Amie had been so distracted by her thoughts as they approached the soldiers that she hadn't noticed her sister beginning to falter. And Mara wasn't great at knowing her limits—or if she was, she wasn't great at admitting them.

Amie moved under her sister's arm, keeping her upright. "Are you alright?"

Teeth gritted, Mara nodded.

"Look," the soldier said. "I don't want to interrupt your travels or make any assumptions, but I thought you both might need a rest."

"If it's not too much trouble," Amie said, "perhaps we could sit with you for a short while."

The soldier nodded and moved to assist Amie in helping Mara to the camp. Saleh followed, tentatively picking his footing as he crossed onto uneven ground. The other two soldiers stood to make room for the sisters. One of them had a bloodstained cloth wrapped around his shoulder while the other appeared to be healthy, though rattled enough for the three of them.

Amie and the soldier eased Mara into place before he addressed them again. "My name is Rossok." He pointed to the injured soldier. "That's Tarub." He pointed to his other companion. "And that's Normand."

"I'm Amie, and this is my sister, Mara. And our horse, Saleh."

Normand smiled at her and pulled his pack close. "Would you girls like something to eat? I have some dried meat you can try while we cook."

Amie nodded. "I'd like that, thank you."

Normand looked at Mara. "And for you?"

Mara shook her head. "Do you have water?"

Tarub grabbed a waterskin from beside him and passed it to Mara. Mara took it with a half-hearted smile of appreciation and drank greedily.

Rossok's eyebrows raised as he watched Mara drink. "I take it you girls have been out here a while."

"A while," Mara confirmed as she finally relinquished the waterskin to Amie.

"Hopefully, we're headed in the same direction," Rossok continued. "Where'd you say you're from?"

"We didn't," Amie said. "We're from Azuri."

Tarub and Normand shared a look. Amie didn't know what to make of it, but she knew it was somehow the wrong answer.

"And you?"

"We're headed to Azuri, too," Rossok said. "Or, at least,

we plan to stop there." He nodded to the injured soldier. "That's where Tarub's from."

"Oh?" Amie said. "What part?"

Tarub glanced at Rossok before answering. "Well, I'm not exactly from inside the town. . . ."

"The outskirts then?" Amie asked.

Tarub nodded. "Right. We don't go to town often."

"If you don't mind my asking," Rossok said as he squatted to help Normand with unpacking their food reserves. "How'd you two come to be out here?"

"We were ca—"

"It's a long story," Amie said, cutting her sister off. "I'm sure you wouldn't want to hear it."

"I very much doubt that," Rossok said. "Your sister looks like she might faint, your horse has a limp, and you're both dressed like—"

"Do you have a spare cloak?" Amie asked. "Or two?"

Normand shook his head. "No. We only have the uniforms we're wearing. Everything else got lost in the fray."

As the soldiers began preparing their meal, Amie moved to care for Saleh. She hadn't managed to procure a brush after she and Mara had escaped captivity, so she took to the tedious, near-impossible process of hand grooming him. It wasn't all bad though. More so than their steady walk south, the grooming process did more to mute the vision of her father's dead eyes, his body lying in the prison cart. Mara had never been one for conversation—at least with her—and in the absence of much else to do but walk, her mind inevitably found its way back to the most recent and horrific trauma she'd ever experienced.

She wondered if the pain ever dimmed. If one day she might wake up and find that it hurt just one touch less. If she could ever think of him and smile rather than weep.

"You both look so much alike," Amie heard Rossok say. She glanced back to see him plop down next to Mara with a damp cloth and place it on her forehead. "And are both beautiful. Tell me. Are either of you courting anyone?"

Amie almost snorted a laugh. Father didn't let boys within ten feet of either of them. Not that Mara needed him to set any such boundary. Most of the time, she acted as if boys didn't even exist. She preferred to study the books that Gavini had loaned her or write in her room when she wasn't working for Father.

A pang of sorrow rang through her bones. *Father.*

"Please," Mara said. "I appreciate your kind service, but spare me your advances. I've heard them all—every turn of phrase and innuendo—and no man is as clever as he thinks himself."

Tarub and Normand shook with laughter, and Rossok grinned, taking Mara's sting in stride. "Come now, you couldn't have heard them all. You must have dozens of suitors to have heard so many."

"My father owned a tavern," Mara said simply. "I've heard better advances than you could possibly think of on your own."

"Owned?" Rossok said. "He doesn't own it anymore?"

Amie found that she had suddenly completed enough of Saleh's grooming for the evening, and gave him a gentle rub on the nose before she turned and crossed back to the camp. "So, Rossok, what does your family do? I mean, when you're not fighting a war?"

The soldier pulled his gaze away from her sister and glared at Amie before he softened his eyes with a smile. "If I told you that, I'd have to kill you."

"Is it that illegal?" Amie asked as she took a seat next to Mara.

"No. It's just so very uninteresting that if you knew about it, fine girls such as yourselves would immediately grow bored of me. And I can't have you spreading rumors about the truth." He gave her a wink.

Amie lifted her brow to mask the fact that she really

wanted to scowl. *He's hiding something.* She didn't know what or why, but there was more to these soldiers than what they were letting on. "And you two? What do you do?"

Normand shifted uncomfortably. "My father farms."

"And my father is a mason." Tarub said.

"A mason that rarely comes into town?" Amie said with as much innocence as she could muster. "He should really consider coming in to talk to some of the business owners. There's a lot of work to be done and few mason families to do it. He could stand to make quite the coin."

"He was injured several years back," Tarub said, glancing away.

"But I'm sure he taught you the trade."

Tarub met her gaze for a brief moment. "Yes, but now that I'm injured, I doubt I will be able to work for quite some time."

"Well, keep it in mind," Amie said. "I'll be sure to let a few of the local shop owners know about your skill. There will be plenty of need when you're ready in several months. And I know Father will want some work done to the new inn he wants to buy."

Mara looked at her then. "What—"

Amie breathed a shy giggle and gripped her sister's hand with just enough pressure to quiet her. "I know I shouldn't be speaking for Father. He probably doesn't want too many people knowing he's getting back into the business."

"Well," Rossok said. "You girls are welcome to travel with us. It's a long road, and who knows what men might be out here?"

Amie gave him a pleasant smile. "We appreciate your assistance this evening but we should—"

Rossok raised a hand, cutting her off. "Now, I know you don't want to be a burden. But we really wouldn't feel right about leaving you two out here on your own. Your sister and horse are hurt. That's not good odds."

"Perhaps there is something we can do to repay you for your services," Mara said.

"The chance to travel with two cultured and beautiful women is payment enough," Rossok said. "And I'm sure your father will be generous with Tarub." He leaned in. "If he keeps that arm."

"We'll accept your assistance," Mara said.

"Mara—"

"The kind soldier is correct," Mara said, looking to her sister. "The road is long, and we are at quite the disadvantage. If we work together, making camp every night will be easier, and the road will be smoother."

"It's settled then!" Rossok said and passed them both a bowl of rice. "Bargain struck."

Amie accepted the bowl and thanked Normand for cooking. She and her sister sat silently as the soldiers began to recount some of the battle for the two of them, making every effort to spare them the details that might kill their appetite.

But Amie's deep feeling of unease with the three kept her from enjoying what would easily qualify as a decent bard's tale. She watched as they met eyes before changing details, paused before reconsidering the reveal of a name.

They were hiding something. Not just Rossok. And they were all in on it together.

THREE

THE FARM

Amie barely slept that night. The small clearing off the North Hzorah road was hardly large enough for them to spread out, and Normand had slept too close to her backside for comfort. When she didn't feel him breathing on the back of her neck, she could hear his snoring directly in her ear. How Amie ended up as the buffer between Mara and the three soldiers, she didn't know, but next time it would be Mara's turn.

And then there was the issue of what the soldiers were actually up to. Why were they alone instead of with the rest of the army? What was it that they were hiding? Why were they so interested in Amie and her sister?

She didn't know much about an army or if them being out here alone was normal—the battle was over after all—but wouldn't they have happened upon a dozen other groups instead of this one solitary trio?

As the night gave way to morning and the sun's warm rays implored them to continue their journey to Azuri, the soldiers rose, packed up camp, and continued down the long road. Amie, Mara, and Saleh trailed just behind them. Twice now, Amie had tried to slow enough that the soldiers would fall out of earshot, but the men interpreted that as the girls needing a break. And so, Amie couldn't snatch a moment with Mara to discuss her intuition.

Not that Mara would listen. Amie could almost hear her sister's arguments already: "What you feel and what is are often distinct," or "Are we really in a position to reject their assistance?" Both were arguments Amie would have a hard time rebutting.

Just ahead, Rossok raised a hand, bringing the soldiers and sisters to a halt. "There's someone ahead."

"It's likely just a farmer," Mara said. "There are dozens of small farms here in the north."

Rossok turned back to them. "Maybe we should flag them down. Perhaps they could help us with some supplies."

Tarub gave a single nod. "I wouldn't mind a new bandage."

"And our food rations are dangerously low," Normand said in agreement. He looked toward Amie and Mara. "Not that we don't want you along—"

Mara waved a hand. "No. You're right. Stopping would be wise."

As if a consensus hadn't already been reached, they each turned to Amie. She sighed and crossed her arms. "I suppose you're all right."

Rossok put on a small but handsome smile of thanks before he turned and jogged ahead, whistling and waving his arms to catch the attention of a man riding along with his horses as they carted hay from one field to another. The man stopped the cart as Rossok approached and listened as he gestured about and described their situation.

Tarub looked at Mara. "Perhaps they have something for our pain."

"Hopefully they have spice berries," Mara said. "That will help treat your infection. They won't do much for me, but they are mildly analgesic."

Tarub raised his eyebrows in surprise. "I thought your father was an innkeeper, not a healer."

Before Mara could respond, Amie interjected. "You'd be surprised how often someone stumbles into the inn with a broken arm or an awful gash. And there is the occasional brawl after a bit too much ale. It's useful to know a little of what the local medicine house knows."

"They're coming," Normand said.

Rossok trotted back toward them as the man followed with his cart. "He says to hop in the back of the cart!" he called ahead. "It'll make getting to the farm easier."

Mara's shoulders dropped in relief as the farmer stopped just before them and hopped down to help. He wasn't a very tall man, but was broad and looked strong. He helped Amie up into the hay-filled cart with ease and half-lifted Mara after.

"My name is Eli," the farmer said as he secured Saleh's reins to the cart. "The ride will be bumpy, but it ain't nothing too fierce."

"Saleh is injured." Amie pointed to their horse. "Hurt his leg on the journey. Please go slow for his sake."

Eli nodded as if finally understanding what had gone so terribly wrong. "Yes, ma'am."

And with that, he hopped back into the cart's box seat and urged his two-horse team on. Saleh plodded along just beside the cart as they turned into the farmer's field, and the five of them arranged themselves to be as comfortable as possible amongst the rough hay.

Soon, the cart pulled into a clearing where an unexpectedly large house and barn waited to greet them. Several chickens clucked as they flitted out of the way of the farmer's cart, and a girl that was roughly Amie's age paused her cranking of the pulley over a well when she spotted that Eli hadn't come alone. She quickly finished raising the bucket, tied it in place, then lifted her skirts as she crossed the distance to greet the unexpected travelers.

"Father!" she called. "I didn't know we were expecting visitors. Mother will have to—"

"Me neither," Eli said. "Help me get our guests inside, Leanna. They're weary from traveling and got nothing but the clothes on their backs."

As Eli and Leanna helped Tarub off the cart, Amie helped her sister. Mara didn't seem to need much of a hand, however. Amie was glad for that. An independent Mara was a healthy Mara. A good sign.

Rossok pointed to the well and gave Leanna a warm smile. "Mind if I carry the pail in for you, Lady Leanna?"

Leanna immediately blushed. "I'm not a lady, but I appreciate the offer and gladly accept."

Amie was surprised to hear a completely different accent from Leanna than her father. The North Hzorah drawl was always a stark contrast from West Hzorah's posh, Ehrel-influenced lilt, and Leanna sounded as if she'd lived her entire life in Azuri instead of out here in the countryside, just south of the Shadow Peaks.

Amie and Mara followed Eli and Leanna into the house while Tarub and Normand took up the rear. Inside was a large drawing room that seemed to have been repurposed as a place to sort and mend a variety of clothing and store an assortment of supplies. Leanna rushed to scoop up piles of clothes as she entered.

"I apologize," Eli said. "We don't entertain many guests and the past few days have been rather busy 'round here."

"Think nothing of it," Rossok said as he set the water bucket on the floor. "Where do you want it?"

Five women flooded into the room, followed by two other men—one quite old, and another near Mara's age. The young man took the pail with a smile and said, "I'll take it off your hands. Thank you for your help," before he carried it back into the house.

"Ah," Eli said. "This is my family. My mother and father," he said and pointed to the older man and woman. "My wife, Dasi, and our three daughters: Versi, Ryla, and Leanna, who you've already met."

Each of them offered a kind wave as their names were called and a warm welcome after Eli finished introducing them. The younger man re-entered the room and stood beside Versi, and Eli crossed over to him and clasped him on the back. "And this is my son-in-law, Marek."

Versi took Marek's arm. "Not *yet*, Father."

Eli winked at them. "They're marrying next week, and I'm just trying to get used to the privilege of calling him that. Never had a son." He wiped his brow in mock relief. "Ain't never wanted one. But Marek won me over after I saw what he could do with a plow."

"Father!" Versi exclaimed. "Don't be crass! It really is good to meet you."

Rossok raised his hand. "I'm Rossok. That's Tarub and Normand. We three are Hzorah soldiers. These two are Mara and Amie, sisters from Azuri."

"Versi," Eli said. "Can you and the girls take the good soldier and these fine young women out back and treat their injuries while I get some ale? Marek, can you stable the horses?"

"Ours hurt its leg," Amie piped in. "Please be careful with him."

Marek nodded in acknowledgment and Eli's wife, Dasi, ushered the women and Tarub deeper into the house and into a fair-sized storeroom just off of the home's kitchen. The room appeared to double as the family's dining room with a long table stretched along the length of the rear wall.

Leanna appraised Mara and Amie before guiding them to sit. "Your travels must have been dreadful!" She turned to the youngest—Ryla, a girl who'd seen perhaps twelve years. "Can you fetch these girls something to wear? They can't continue on in this state."

As Ryla hurried up a flight of stairs, Dasi took to preparing a salve, guiding Leanna in the process while Versi and Eli's mother assisted Tarub in removing his leather armor. After they peeled back the red and brown stained cloth, Versi's frown grew tight.

"I need to wash this," Dasi said.

Unphased, Tarub said, "Do what you must."

Versi poured a bit of the well water that had been brought back into the room into a basin, then set the remaining water by the rear door. She pointed to where several differing arrowheads were affixed to the wall. "What kind of arrow is inside of you?"

Tarub looked at the line of arrows but shook his head. "I don't know. Does it matter?"

"It matters," Dasi said. "Some arrows do more damage on the way out than on the way in. And those that do all have different methods."

Tarub swallowed. "Should we leave it in then?"

Dasi waved a hand. "No, no. It must come out. It'll just take a bit more effort to discover what's inside before I give it a good tug."

"I imagine that means more pain."

"Eh," Dasi said as she examined the wound. "I prefer you not imagine it first." She turned to her mother-in-law. "I'll need a hand."

Ryla descended the stairs with two bundles of light brown dresses. "I hope these will fit well." She glanced at Tarub before adding, "Come out back with me? We can try them on."

When Tarub gave them a nod that said he'd be just fine alone, Amie and Mara followed Ryla out the back door and onto a small porch. Amie stepped out of her nightshift and kicked it into a corner, and Ryla lugged the bucket of water outside.

"There's a clean washcloth behind you if you'd like to wash before you redress," Ryla said.

Amie was so happy that she almost drew Ryla into a hug, but only just restrained herself. "That sounds wonderful. Thank you!"

Ryla smiled before stepping back into the house to give the sisters a moment of privacy. As soon as the door snapped shut, Amie turned to her sister. "We need to talk."

Mara freed herself of her nightshift, drenched the gray washcloth, and took to washing away the dirt and sweat. "I hadn't noticed."

"These soldiers," Amie said, beginning to bathe as well, "they're hiding something."

"Go on," Mara said without pausing her wash.

"They went out of their way to flag us down and insisted we travel with them," Amie said. "They kept asking personal questions, and only gave answers that we practically handed to them."

Mara—still focused on her grooming—didn't look to her, but she did snort a small laugh. "So, they're hiding something because they're kind and interested?"

"No," Amie said. "They're hiding something because they're *hiding* something."

"Mmm." Mara shimmied into the new dress and slipped on a pair of well-worn, soft leather shoes.

"'Mmm?' Is that all you have to say?"

"Yes." Mara's gaze narrowed as she looked to the field beyond the farm.

"Really?" Amie had just about had enough. Somehow, her sister always knew exactly how to drive her to anger. And nothing made her angrier than when Mara refused to take her seriously. "This is important. What if—"

Before Amie could finish, Mara grabbed her shift, hopped off the porch, and marched into the field behind the farm house.

"Wait!" Amie cried out as she pulled on her shoes and gave chase.

Unlike the rows of crops that had populated the farm's entry, the rear had been reserved for cattle. Stretched over a relatively flat expanse of pasture, black and brown cows peppered the land, casually grazing on thick, green grass.

Mara ignored the cattle, and the cattle, for the most part, ignored her as she continued through the field before she stopped by a rather large—and foul—pile of manure.

Amie had to jog to catch up with Mara's determined charge. She held her nose as the fumes overwhelmed her senses. "I'd ask what you're doing by this Desolate-bound pile of horrid defecate, but I'm sure there's no explanation that wouldn't fail the test of sanity."

Mara squatted low and pointed. "I saw them glistening in the sunlight."

Amie lowered herself to her sister's level to see what she was pointing at. Atop the moist manure was a layer of white crystals. "What is that?"

"Niter," Mara said.

"Right," Amie said. "Niter. So, about these soldiers . . ."

"I heard what you said," Mara growled while she placed her nightshift on the ground.

"Are you sure? Because it seems like you're not—" Amie gasped. "Mara, you dolt! That's *disgusting*!"

Mara had begun scraping the niter off of the manure and into her shift. Once she'd collected about two handfuls, she drew the shift together and tied it to form a small, gross pouch.

"I didn't know city girls liked dung so much," a voice called from behind them.

Amie turned to see Versi and Ryla walking toward them from the house. Mara slowly rose to stand next to her sister then held up her nightshift pouch.

"You don't mind, do you?" Mara asked. "I apologize. I should have asked before I collected it, but I was so taken with the novelty, I couldn't help myself. Our town expends a lot of effort to keep out streets clear of manure, and my father never allowed me to use our stables as a testing ground to grow any niter."

Versi looked as perplexed as Amie felt, but eventually, she shrugged as she and her younger sister stopped before them. "Think nothing of it. We collect the dung here from the cattle and eventually cart it off to another part of the farm."

"The dresses fit you well!" Ryla said. "The shoes aren't much, but we don't keep many spares."

"We're just glad to finally have something on our feet," Amie said. "I never thought I'd appreciate shoes so much."

"Do you use the crystals for your crops?" Mara asked.

Versi cocked her head, and Ryla looked up at Mara, confused. "No. Why would we?"

As if she had seen the most beautiful flower in existence, a smile spread across Mara's face. "I assume you're using above-ground irrigation, allowing gravity the carry water downhill and through your trenches?"

Versi gave a small smile. "Are you sure you're from Azuri?"

"Are you from the country?" Amie interjected, her curiosity getting the better of her. "You and your sisters have completely different accents from your parents."

"We're from here," Versi confirmed. "But our mother spent some time in West Hzorah, and it lightened her North Hzorah accent considerably. She was the one who tutored us, and so, naturally, we took to her way more so than Father's."

"Huh."

"So," Mara said, with a sharp glare at her sister. "You can use niter to promote crop growth. I would recommend grinding it to a finer grain, then evenly salting your fields with it. I'm assuming the irrigation system you use is based on rain runoffs from the Shadow Peaks rather than your well water."

Versi nodded. "The runoffs make several streams throughout the north, but only fill in the spring when it gets warm and even more after the rains."

"I'd recommend waiting until it looks like rain is imminent," Mara said, nodding to herself as she thought it through. "Salting your crops with niter is best when there's enough water to dissolve the grains and increase the needed elements to your crops."

Amie rolled her eyes as the two continued to discuss how to best fertilize their crops before turning to Ryla. "What do you do for fun around here?"

Ryla smiled. "I have a hideout where I keep all my treasures. Want to see?"

"Now that sounds fun," Amie said and followed Ryla away from Mara's droll explanations.

She turned back to look at the house a moment and wondered if the soldiers would convince the farmers to help them with a few supplies before they had to head out again.

FOUR

THE ARROWHEAD

Tarub tested the limits of his new but limited range of motion in his shoulder. He winced in pain as he found the extent of his flexibility. And it wasn't broad.

"I wouldn't do that," the old one said as she rinsed her tools in a shallow basin.

She had a kind way about her—the way his own grandmother had. It made him want more than anything to see her again. But he couldn't. At least, not until the Creed took back Hzorah or Titan returned to set things right. And even then, he may never see her. Would Titan grant him that? Would he recognize how tired Tarub was? How afraid he was?

No, a voice whispered from the depths of fear. *You don't deserve it. That arrow should have killed you on the spot. At least then you would have died honorably*.

"You," Leanna said, as she helped Tarub off the farmhouse's kitchen table, "are the bravest and most honorable man I have ever met. You took an arrow for Hzorah. And you didn't even cry out when my nene took it out of you."

Tarub forced a smile past another pang of guilt. "Your nene has gifted hands. I didn't feel a thing."

The old one looked to him, her eyes alight with good humor. "My hands ain't any more gifted than any other woman. It's Desolate's Hand you should thank. If you'd gotten it in your head to take out that arrowhead, the wound wouldn't have clotted, and you would have died."

"Thank Desolate's Hand then," Tarub said, the heathen words grating against his now blasphemous tongue. "Can I see it?"

The old one nodded to her granddaughter, and Leanna stepped away before returning with a tin pan. She rattled it and giggled, pretending that the arrowhead had a mind of its own.

"I think it wants to get back in you." She put her ear to the pan. "Yes. . . . Yes. It says it's too cold out here."

Her grandmother swatted her behind with a towel, and Tarub grinned as he took the pan and stared down at the dark gray arrowhead. Jagged teeth ridged its sharp edges, and the initials of its maker were etched into the arrowhead's flat side. The craftsmanship was exceptional. Like Dasi had feared, it was designed to hurt more on the way out than it did on the way in, and Tarub could testify to the maker's skill.

"Can I keep it?" Tarub asked, looking to the old one.

Dasi shrugged and lifted a thumb to the wall of arrowheads. "No good keeping it here. We have one like it in our collection already, and I think it'll make a fine trophy for you."

After Tarub tucked the arrowhead away in his trousers, he thanked Dasi, Leanna, and the old one for her help, then stood and made his way back into the front room where Rossok and Normand sat with the farmer, his father-in-law, and his daughter's betrothed.

"And that," Rossok said in grand fashion, "is when I realized there were two men I knew I could count on without question." He paused as Tarub entered the room and held out a hand as if he were introducing Tarub for the very first time. "And there's one of them. The man who took an arrow for me."

Tarub winced a smile as Rossok clapped him on the back. Rossok offered him a seat and Tarub took it. Sitting was the best way to keep his shoulder from moving too much. The medicine had begun its work in dulling the pain, but he could still feel the sting from the arrow's entry and the burn from his newly-threaded stitches.

"I know you got a fine tale too," Eli said, looking to Normand. "You're quiet, but ain't it the quiet ones that got the most to say?"

Normand waved his hands in protest, but Rossok spoke up. "Don't be shy, Normand. Tell him what you did. How you protected our squad from certain death."

Normand, of course, had done no such thing. His face paled as he sputtered, trying to follow Rossok's quick tongue. "I . . . Well, you see, it wasn't so straightforward as all that. I—"

"It was an hour or so past midday," Rossok interjected. "It's hard to be sure exactly what time it was. Time doesn't mean much out there. Our squad was tasked with cutting to the heart of the Creed's army to strike down their general, but the ring of soldiers that protected him was fierce and finding our way close was a trial if I ever had one.

"As we drew near—*bam!*" Rossok clapped his hands together. "Another squad slammed into us, taking one of my men down with them. We recovered quickly, but not quick enough. Only Normand had the wits to respond."

Tarub listened in astonishment as Rossok continued to fabricate an entire scene of battlefield carnage. The tale was so well told that Tarub almost bought into the idea that it had really happened. Tarub had always known Rossok was clever and a great soldier, but he never realized how good of a storyteller he was. It was as if lying was the most natural thing in the world for him.

At the end of Rossok's story, the farmers congratulated

Normand for his bravery. Normand, clearly uncomfortable with the undeserved praise, bowed his head in shame, but it must have looked like humble appreciation, for the farmers beckoned him to hold his head high.

Then Eli turned to Tarub. "I see my mother-in-law got your poultice and bandages set. You won't have a full range of motion for a while, but take it slow, and eventually, you'll heal up. You young folk always do."

"We should really allow them to stay here," Marek, the oldest daughter's fiancé, said. "That wound won't do well out on the road, and they deserve some rest."

Rossok held up his hands in protest. "We couldn't possibly—"

"Nonsense," Eli said. "Y'all are more than welcome at my home. Heroes for Hzorah are always welcome."

Marek nodded, eagerly. "One of my best friends was drafted to fight. I haven't heard from him since. Maybe you knew him? His name was Mel."

Rossok shook his head. "No, I don't know him."

He looked to Tarub and Normand, but they didn't know him either. Tarub swallowed hard. There was a very good chance that Mel had died. After the beasts from the sky had attacked and frozen the ground, many had died.

The three of them hadn't come up with an explanation for what had happened out there on the battlefield. But Normand had offered the only plausible reason: Titan's grace. The beasts attacked the Hzorah army and largely skirted groups of the Creed's soldiers. And Rossok had said that he wasn't sure they'd be alive if it wasn't for the ice creatures.

Marek gave a short nod. "I suppose the army was large. He's probably right behind you two."

Tarub had known Rossok for some time now, and his glance to them after Marek's reply was all too clear. They couldn't stay.

If Marek's friend had survived the early moments of the

battle, what had saved the Creed was likely what had ended the Hzorah soldier, but they couldn't stay on that assumption alone. That would risk the inconvenient revelation that they were soldiers of the Creed when—if—his friend returned home.

"Look," Rossok said. "We don't want to be a bother, and we would love to get home and see our families as soon as we can. We should really get back on the road as soon as possible."

"Of course, of course!" Eli said. "I can't hold you back from your families. They ain't seen you in weeks. Must be worried sick."

Rossok nodded. "Exactly. And I promised Mother I'd get back as fast as my feet would carry me."

Tarub looked at Rossok with a raised brow. He hadn't counted on Rossok being so good at talking his way into the hearts of those around him. *Is that what happened to me? Did I abandon the Creed because of Rossok? Is that what I really wanted, or did he make me think that's what I wanted?*

It was unsettling, doubting his own resolve, but he'd plunged headfirst into a new life now. He'd have to grapple with his insecurities later when they found safety.

"Before you head out," Eli said, looking to Tarub, "can I see it?"

Tarub blinked in confusion. "See it?"

Eli nodded with a smile. "The arrowhead that you took for your friend. You kept it, didn't you?"

Tarub nodded hesitantly. "Yes."

"Go on then," Rossok said. "Let him see it."

Tarub eased himself out of the chair and crossed the room. He fished the arrowhead out of his pocket and dropped it into Eli's outstretched hand. Tarub settled back into the chair, and Eli leaned forward to examine it.

"Mmm," the farmer said. "Interesting. Beautiful."

"It didn't feel beautiful going in," Tarub said.

Eli chuckled and met Tarub's eyes. "I'm sure it didn't. I'm sure. Marek, come look at this."

The young man leaned toward Eli and took the arrowhead from him. After flipping it over in his fingers for a moment, he glanced up at the three of them, taking each of them in. He then passed it to the old man who scrutinized the arrowhead with the strained eyes of old age.

Rossok leaned forward. "Is there something wrong?"

Eli sat back in his chair. "Nothing's wrong. But I'm curious. Where in Hzorah did you say you're from?"

"Azuri," Normand piped in.

"Yes, I know that," Eli said with a smile before turning his attention back to Rossok. "You told me that he's from Azuri and you two got to drop him off there. But what about you? Where are you from?"

Tarub watched Rossok as he slowly frowned. "About a day's travel south of Azuri. It's not a town. You wouldn't even know of the place with it so tucked away as it is."

"On the countryside?" Eli asked.

Rossok nodded. "That's right."

"Interesting."

"Interesting?"

"Your accent," Eli said, rubbing his chin. "Knife to my throat, I'd swear up and down that you ain't got a drop of West Hzorah blood in you. Those girls are for sure from West Hzorah, but you three . . . You three ain't."

Tarub glanced at Normand, and his jaw tightened as he felt his skin flush.

"Now hold on a second." Rossok raised a hand. "I think you have us all wrong—"

Eli let out a low whistle and a chuckle as he gestured for the old man to hand him the arrowhead. "I'm a farmer, and I'll admit I'm a bit slow on the uptake sometimes lessen I got a good teacher. But I'm a far cry from stupid. My wife spent her whole life in Azuri before I up and stole her away to the country life. I know a West Hzorah accent when I hear it, and you ain't got it."

Rossok sat up straighter. "I think you may not be familiar with—"

"What I believe," Eli interrupted, "is that y'all got spooked by the battle on the plains and thought it smart to switch sides. You found and dressed yourselves in uniforms from a few fallen Hzorah troops, and made off like you were in the Hzorah army all along."

The farmer twiddled the arrowhead between his fingers, waiting for Rossok to respond to his accusation, but Rossok merely raised his brow as if curious to hear more. Pleased with Rossok's invitation to continue, Eli went on.

"Now, I ain't got a clue about those Azuri girls. Don't know why they're out this way alone or how y'all met. They might be too scared to run or speak up for themselves after you captured them, but I reckon they don't even know who you are."

Tarub swallowed hard. They'd been found out. He almost felt sick with fear as he fought to remain calm against the sudden burst of energy in his veins. But Rossok's stonewalled expression didn't change as he held the farmer's eyes, his thumb stroking the pommel of his sword.

"It seems to me that you've made a big leap based on the way we talk," Rossok said.

Eli nodded. "That could be. But that ain't the whole of what gave you away." He held up the arrowhead, admiring it. "I got a friend who got a good commission recently. There ain't been such a demand for quality arrows for a long time, and he had to hire two dozen farmers to help him make enough for the army. He taught me to appreciate the craftsmanship of a well-made arrow—how every arrow maker has their own signature design. This arrowhead is his make." Eli's casual expression suddenly shifted to an intense glower as he looked at Tarub. "You were shot by the side you claim to be on."

Rossok sat still for a moment before he sat back in his chair. "Well then, it appears you have it all figured out. What do you mean to do with us?"

"I won't treat you poorly," Eli said. "I ain't never felt it my place to pass judgment, and I don't mean to start now. I think you boys are good people trying to do something right for once, trying to find a new life. I ain't got nothing against that, and I'll speak on your behalf, but we got to do this the right way. We'll let you stay locked in the barn. We'll bring you food and water, of course. There's sure to be many other soldiers that will pass through. When they do, I'll let them decide what to do with you based on the king's directives."

"Mmm," Rossok mused, rubbing his chin. "Not ideal."

"No," Eli said, "but it's the only right way."

"I think I'll have to pass up on your offer," Rossok said.

"Now, I—"

Before the farmer could finish, Rossok lept to his feet and drew his sword in the same motion. The farmer was quick to respond and the two clashed when Eli pulled an iron fire stoker from beside his chair and parried Rossok's deadly thrust.

With the flash of a dagger, young Marek leapt to the farmer's defense, but Normand had gained his guts and tackled him. They crashed onto a wooden table, scattering an assortment of ceramic dishes. Tarub—his pain forgotten in the chaos—found his feet just as Rossok took Eli by his shirt and swung him in his direction. It was all Tarub could do to leap out of the way.

As Tarub fell to the hard, wooden floor, his shoulder pain re-invited itself to the forefront of his mind. He gritted his teeth against the searing pain as he maneuvered himself against the far wall. Marek wasn't undone by Normand's attack, and somehow, he'd kicked the soldier off, pushing Normand several paces across the room while propelling himself over the small table. He landed with a heavy thud, and his dagger clattered to the floor.

Just in front of Tarub.

Without a thought, Tarub snatched the dagger and turned to Marek's writhing form. He skidded across the floor, ignoring his shoulder's fiery sting. And before Marek could mount a recovery, he drove the dagger into the boy's throat. He turned away, only just managing to skirt a majority of the spray of blood.

Panting with relief, Tarub rolled away from Marek's final gurgling breaths to see Rossok pull his sword out of the farmer's gut. Close-mouthed, Rossok drew in two slow, angry breaths before using the sleeve of his Hzorah uniform to smear away the blood on his cheeks.

Then, with one last calming breath, he turned to the old man. Eli's father stood against the wall, frozen in fear with nothing to defend himself but the length of one of his granddaughters' dresses that had somehow gotten soiled in the mayhem. Rossok took his time crossing the room, staring deep into the old man's tearing eyes.

Rossok, his stance unnervingly still, watched the man as he trembled under the shadow of his enemy. For a moment, Tarub thought Rossok might turn away. But as soon as the thought came to him, Rossok struck, cleaving the man's throat. The old one collapsed, and Rossok stepped aside as the man fell forward onto shards of shattered dishes.

FIVE

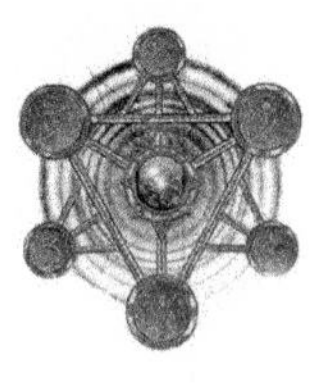

ESCAPE

Mara watched as Amie and Ryla reappeared in the distance, stepping high to clear the tall grass that was inaccessible by the farm's cattle, and it suddenly struck her how much older her sister had become. Ryla, a girl who'd seen no more than ten years looked a child next to Amie. Amie had seen sixteen years now and had passed the threshold of womanhood. Still, she hadn't quite recognized it until the contrast was so plain before her.

After her mother had died, she'd tried to ease her father's worries by helping care for Amie as much as possible so that he was free to manage the Kruv House, but he had always been there—a real parent. Now that their father had died after the Dominion soldiers attacked their tavern and captured them, Mara had begun to fear what that meant for Amie. Without him, she alone was responsible for her sister.

Proximity without respite had a way of warping one's view of those you're closest to. Seeing her now, smiling down at the young Ryla, she realized that perhaps she'd been trapped into thinking of her sister as though she were Ryla's age. There were still dangers that youth would inevitably spring upon Amie, but once they were in Caldor with Gavini, Amie would have more than enough to occupy her time and protect her from flights of fancy.

At least we have the Hzorah soldiers to help me keep Amie safe, Mara thought. *At least there's that.*

"Your sister is good with children," Dasi, the farmer's wife, said. She, Leanna, Versi, and the old one sat together on two large bales of hay.

"Apparently so," Mara said.

"She is young, but will make a wonderful mother when the time comes."

Mara managed to refrain from snorting a laugh at the thought of Amie taking on the responsibility of parenthood. "I don't think marriage or children are in our futures. Not any time soon, that is."

"Oh?" the old one asked with a gentle tease. "Your standards for men are so high?"

Mara had never found herself interested in taking a husband and planned to avoid it at all costs. She'd seen nineteen years and was of age to be wed, but she'd developed certain strategies to ward off the interests of young men who frequented her father's establishment. It had taken over a year, but callers for her attention had reduced significantly.

People like her couldn't find fulfillment in marriage.

People like her were better off unwed.

People like her were . . . undesirable.

"Yes," Mara said as she looked away. "I would say that my standards are quite insurmountable. However, I only meant that my father has recently passed into Desolate, and my sister and I will have our hands full with the management of the Kruv House."

Dasi's eyes grew wide. "Your father owned the Kruv House?"

Mara nodded. "Yes. You knew of it?"

"Knew of it? You'd be pressed to find a man or woman from West Hzorah who hadn't heard of it, at least in passing." Dasi suddenly withdrew her wonder as the realization of Mara's words hit her. "I am very sorry for your loss."

Mara wasn't unaware of her father's popularity. However, she'd only *heard* that he and the Kruv House were popular. She had never ventured far from Azuri and therefore, had no real evidence that the stories were true. And in some small measure, knowing that his life had been appreciated made his passing feel . . . less severe.

"I do hope word of the Kruv House is upstanding," Mara said, turning the subject away from her grief.

"Your reputation is impeccable," Dasi said. "I wouldn't stay anywhere else if I ever find myself in Azuri."

"You flatter us," Mara said with a small, appreciative smile. "But our good name isn't won passively. We'll have our hands full."

"And that is why you must marry," the farmer's mother said. "Wouldn't it be easier to maintain the Kruv house with a man about? You girls look plenty capable, but there are certain dangers in running such a popular inn. Not to mention how it may look."

Versi nodded in agreement with her grandmother. "Exactly! The way I hear it, your father was but a hair away from Low Lordship. It's probably inevitable that you'd be offered Lordship soon. But without a husband, you won't be able to take the title of Low Lady."

It hadn't really been Mara's plan to take over the Kruv House. She wanted to, but there were matters much larger than her that needed to be attended to. Gavini would need her in Caldor, and that's exactly where she intended to go. However, she didn't think it was wise to tell anyone else her plan. At least not until Aunt Bell agreed to take over the Kruv House. It was likely that it would be her aunt and uncle who would rise to Low Lordship, not her.

"Well, if that's how it must be, then that's how it will be," Mara said. "I don't need to be a Low Lady to continue my father's good work."

Versi and Leanna looked shocked at Mara's dismissal of such a grand opportunity, but the old one smiled with earnest appreciation and said, "It's good to know that you know your own mind. Not many your age do."

As Amie approached with Ryla, the young girl jogged ahead to hop up on the hay bale near her mother.

Amie smiled at the farmer's wife. "Your daughter is lovely. She has an adventurous spirit!"

Before Dasi could reply, a crash from the house caught their attention. The women all turned to the house and watched it for a moment, searching for signs of danger. Quiet filled the air as they listened for another sign of trouble, but when none came, Mara turned to Dasi.

"Perhaps we should go inside and check on them."

The house's rear door crashed open and Rossok stumbled on the home's deck. "Mara! Amie!" he called as he spotted the two girls. "Come quick!"

Without a moment's hesitation, Mara was on her feet and running with the other women in close pursuit. A number of catastrophes shuffled through Mara's head as she sprinted, each only just barely touching her awareness before it was pushed aside for another equally unwelcome emergency. As she dashed through the doorway, Rossok tried to grasp her arm, but she slipped from his grip as she made for the sitting room door.

When Mara pushed open the door to the sitting room she froze, shocked at the gruesome scene before her. Clothing, blood, and broken dishes were strewn across the floor, a horrific background to the three men that lay lifeless amongst them. And Normand and Tarub sat against the wall near the front door, panting.

Mara turned back to Rossok's grave stare. His jaw clenched as Amie pushed past him and just barely stopped in time to keep from pushing Mara over. Amie gasped as she took in the scene and backed away.

Mara grabbed Amie's shoulder. "Amie. Don't let the girls see this. Don't let them inside."

A hand over her mouth, Amie nodded before turning to catch the farmer's family just as they filed into the kitchens.

Mara pulled Rossok into the sitting room and shut them inside before she whirled to face him. "What happened here? How—"

"Look," Rossok interrupted. "We didn't have a choice. When we found out about them, they attacked. We tried to reason with them but they wouldn't stop. We had to."

"What?" Mara's grimace drew deeper. "Why did they attack you? What did you find out?"

Rossok pulled a small, brown leather strap from his pocket. "Their prayer belts. Their loyalties are with the Creed. When we found this hidden under the clothes stacked on the table, they attacked."

Mara turned to the other two men beside the door. They each nodded, confirming Rossok's story. She could hardly believe it. The family had been so welcoming and kind. Was it all some trap to lure them into a false sense of security?

"Look," Rossok said as he took Mara by the shoulders and turned her back to him. "We've got to get out of here. They may have been loyal to the Creed, but we will have certainly outstayed our welcome." He looked past Mara to Tarub and Normand. "I say we take what we can and run before the family gets the locals involved."

Mara frowned. "But shouldn't we—"

"No!" Rossok's grip on her shoulder tightened into a painful vice before he remembered himself and let go. "No. They won't understand. They'll just see three soldiers who killed their neighbors. They probably don't even know that they were loyal to the Creed. And if they did, they're probably loyal to the Creed themselves. We managed to fight off these three. But we can't fend off a dozen or so men that come prepared and coordinated."

"That is true," Mara said slowly.

"Good." Rossok, without another moment's consideration, gave a quick signal to his men. Together they leapt into action, grabbing several burlap sacks and shoving supplies inside from a stockpile in the corner of the room.

Mara stepped back into the kitchen, making sure to immediately shut the door behind her. There, Amie stood with her hands outstretched, stuttering as she attempted to come up with an excuse for why the women in the kitchen should see to the men. Mara stepped in front of her. She had to buy them some more time so that the soldiers could prepare for their escape.

"There's been an incident," Mara said as she took in each of their grave expressions. She paused at Dasi. "Your husband . . . He . . . Well, he was caught."

Dasi's expression darkened. "Caught? Caught in what?"

Mara sighed. She'd have to spell it out for them. "The soldiers found out that you are loyal to the Dominion."

"We are no such thing!" Dasi growled and stepped forward. "Let me by!"

Of course, they wouldn't admit to it, Mara thought. *That's a swift way to get yourself ostracized or worse.*

Mara's heart raced as she tried to reason the best way to handle Dasi's anger. Mara wasn't a fighter. If things got physical in the kitchen, Mara worried that she and her sister would not only be at a severe disadvantage because of their inexperience but they were also outnumbered.

"I don't think it would be wise to let your daughters see this," Amie said as she went to her sister's side. "It wouldn't be right."

Realization flooded Dasi's face and she turned to her mother-in-law. They both shared a nod.

"See what?" Ryla asked.

Dasi turned to her young daughter and took her by the hand. "Take your sisters and fetch some more water. Bring it through the back away. We need four or five buckets."

"Five buckets?" Ryla exclaimed. "Why?"

"Now, Ryla!" Dasi said through gritted teeth as she looked to the oldest of the sisters. "Go on now. Quickly. When you're done, stay in the kitchen until I call for you."

Versi came forward and took Ryla by the shoulders and led her and Leanna out of the kitchen. When they were well on their way, Dasi turned back to Mara with tears streaming down her face despite the placid mask she'd put on for her children.

"Are they . . .?"

Mara nodded slowly. "I'm afraid so."

Dasi and the old one broke past Mara and Amie, opened the kitchen door, and stepped inside. A wail of sorrow burst forth from the women, but Mara muffled the sounds as she closed the door behind them and turned to her sister.

"We have to go. Now. Go get Saleh. Hurry!"

SIX

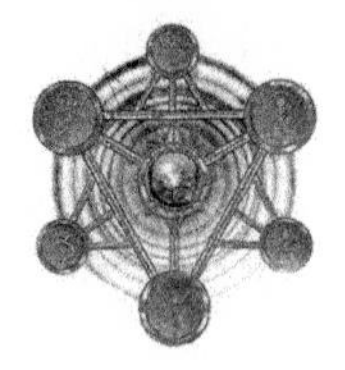

DELIVERERS OF JUSTICE

Tarub gingerly rubbed his shoulder as he watched Normand stir their stew over the fire while Rossok lounged on his side, staring into the starlit expanse. Set off from the path, Tarub wasn't entirely sure they weren't on some other farmer's land, but the clearing was certainly used by travelers in the recent past. A rock-rimmed firepit was set in the ground and fresh firewood had been neatly stacked nearby as if the clearing had expected them to come and wanted their time there to be restful. Sealed vats of vegetables, meat, and broth had been placed nearby under a large, bowing malt tree.

Normand had come to the nervous conclusion that news of the battle's end had begun to reach the people, and that farmers had placed the comforts there to make the journeys of the discharged soldiers easy. Rossok had been elated at their good fortune, barely able to contain himself as he quickly built a fire, uncharacteristically oblivious to how unnerved the rest of them were.

And if I'm feeling this way, Tarub thought as his gaze drifted to Amie and Mara, several dozen paces off where they groomed their horse, *those girls must be shaken to the bone.*

Normand ladled each of them a bowl of stew, but as delicious as the food smelled, Tarub found that he was suddenly uninterested. Still, he forced a few spoonfuls, knowing that he'd regret not eating it later.

"This," Rossok declared with a raised wooden spoon, "is your most brilliant dish so far, Normand!"

Normand looked down at his bowl as he swallowed. "Wasn't really mine."

"Of course it was," Rossok said. "I watched you make it. You should consider becoming a cook. You'll need a new trade in our new life."

"I think he meant that this was meant for the Hzorah soldiers," Tarub said.

Rossok gave them a pointed look. "We *are* Hzorah soldiers. We are whoever we say we are."

"I don't know, Rossok," Normand said. "Those farmers figured us out quick."

"It was the arrow," Rossok said.

"Yes," Normand went on, "but they also knew we had the wrong accents."

"So we don't say we're from West Hzorah," Rossok said.

"Where then?" Normand asked. "We don't know enough of this place to pass for a citizen. We are strangers in the promised land. We never lived here. There is too much we don't know."

"Listen—"

"No!" Normand hissed, taking care not to speak so loudly that the girls would overhear. "No. You listen. You're a great soldier and an excellent liar, but it didn't take long for us to get trapped in our lies! If it's not the arrow, it's our accent. If it's not our accent, it'll be something else. We're fortunate that those girls over there are young enough to believe your bosh."

Rossok stood then. He paced in a small circle before turning back to them. "Maybe you're right. Maybe we can't survive here. But we can't go back. It's too late for that."

Tarub's stomach clenched as he met Rossok and Normand's eyes. Normand was right. Rossok had gotten overconfident when the first people from Hzorah they'd run into were two lost girls. They had believed their story, but the farmers had better sense.

They'd been lucky back at that farmhouse. It had been three trained soldiers against two weaponless farmers and an old man. If it ever came to it again, they may not have as advantageous a confrontation. They couldn't fight their way through every situation. They had to find a place they could be safe.

But Rossok was also right. They couldn't go back now.

"Maybe we don't stay in Hzorah," Tarub said. "Maybe we go somewhere else."

Rossok frowned. "Somewhere else? This is the promised land."

"Yes," Tarub said with a short nod, "but it's no good to us if we die here."

"Where do you propose we go?" Rossok asked.

Tarub shrugged then winced against the pain of his wound. "I don't know. Armoth?"

"Armoth?" Rossok sneered. "With their *queen*? I won't be ruled by a scorching woman. And we don't know the language. We'd be spotted for a Deseran even faster there."

". . . Or Caldor."

"It's destroyed, remember?" Rossok said. "The same beasts that aided us laid waste to the place."

"And there's Ghaya."

"Again," Rossok sighed, "we don't know the language. We couldn't even pass as a Ghayan. They wouldn't even need to hear us speak."

"The Crehn Isles," Normand said, looking up from his bowl. "We could go to the Crehn Isles."

Both Tarub and Rossok looked at Normand, and after a moment, Rossok chuckled. "With the pirates? I thought you were serious for a moment."

"I am serious," Normand said. "It's not just pirates. All sorts of misfits end up there. Thieves and murderers on the run, exiles for one imagined sin or another. Even some of our people must be there."

"Great," Rossok said. "Pirates *and* murderers. We're sure to be safe there."

"*We're* murders, Rossok!"

"We," Rossok said, stepping close to Normand, "are owed this place. This is our land. They stole it from us. We're not murderers. We're deliverers of justice."

Normand didn't look away from Rossok's insistent glare, so Tarub stood. "Maybe Normand's right. We need to go where we can survive. If it's not here and it's not back with the army, then we must find a new place to go. When the war is won, we can come back."

Rossok rubbed his chin as he considered their options. Then he sighed and settled back down near the fire. "Alright. We go to the Crehn Isles."

Normand, looking surprised that he'd won the exchange, merely nodded before whispering, "Good."

The Crehn Isles were a distant land with no real, formal governance. At least, that's what he'd been told as a child. The pirates there visited Janamah often to trade. And while the idea of pirates had always frightened Tarub and riddled his nightmares with episodes of terror, the few times he'd seen pirates, they'd actually been quite civil.

One couldn't always be evil, Tarub supposed. Even the heathens in Hzorah had been accommodating until they learned of their allegiances.

Tarub had never been on a ship before, and the Isles were only accessible by crossing the Great Sea. If he had his way, he would never set foot on a vessel. He'd heard too many stories of fishermen caught in stormy weather and drowning in the cold, inky ocean. He'd have to brave it if he wanted freedom, and again after the war to return to the land that was promised.

It would be worth it. And even if it wasn't, their options were at an end.

Again, he glanced over at the two girls from West Hzorah. They were taking far too long with grooming the horse. No doubt they were discussing what had happened back at the farmhouse. The two girls had probably never seen anything so gruesome.

"What about the girls?" Tarub asked. "We should probably part ways with them. After what's happened, they'd likely welcome the news."

"No," Rossok said as he took up his bowl of stew again. "No. They stay with us."

"But we're going to the Crehn Isles now," Tarub said. "I don't know the land here well, but I know enough that we'll need to head east, not west where they're going."

"They're dumb girls," Rossok said. "They won't know the difference."

"Perhaps," Tarub said. "But it'll be easier to just part ways than try to convince them they're headed home."

Rossok pointed with his wooden spoon. "Those girls are our key out of here. They have a horse. They're young, pretty. That can buy us a lot. That's worth something. And we'll need something to trade if we're to get to the Crehn Isles." He gave them a look of finality. "The girls stay."

It didn't take long before the clear skies twisted with dark clouds, casting the camp in darkness as the moon dimmed behind sheets of rain. It was fortunate that the oak's long arms and summer leaves stretched overhead, shielding Amie from the sudden downpour. She shuddered as a streak of lightning arced across the sky followed by a roar of thunder.

Amie hadn't spoken to Mara since they'd left the farm.

Even now, as Amie groomed Saleh, Mara remained silent, just a pace away, checking the horse's saddle bags for the book they'd taken from Bam Rav. Focused on her work, Mara ensured that the pack would keep the book from water damage.

"It's awful what they did," Mara said, breaking the silence.

Amie nodded. "I agree. They didn't have to kill them."

A look of genuine shock crossed Mara's face. "What? Of course, they did!"

Amie stopped brushing and looked at her sister. "You were talking about the farmers?"

"Yes. Those farmers had it coming. People like them are why we're in this mess to begin with."

"Just because we don't share their beliefs doesn't mean they deserved to die."

"Do you even know what they believe?" Mara asked, hands on her hips.

"I'm not daft," Amie said as she secured Saleh's reins to the tree. "I know they're trying to get the Wizard to return by converting everyone to their religion. I don't believe their Wizard is a god, but that doesn't mean they have to believe the same as we do."

"The problem isn't that they don't believe like us," Mara said through gritted teeth. "The problem is that they're willing to kill us because we don't believe like them!" Mara knelt down and began packing away the supplies that had been gifted to them. "Honestly, Amie, sometimes I don't know if you're putting on or not."

Amie bit her tongue, holding back a scathing retort about her sister's vile and insensitive nature. She didn't like what had happened, but there was some sense to what Mara was saying. She hated how her sister could always make what she felt so deeply seem so utterly foolish.

"I don't think we know what really happened," Amie said.

"I know enough," Mara said as she closed the pack. "And I think I've seen enough blood to last me until I cross into Desolate."

Amie grabbed hold of her sister's arm as she turned back toward the camp. "Mara, listen."

Her sister paused and looked back, though her curt reply was laced with irritation. "Yes?"

"There's something not right about those soldiers. Killing those farmers wasn't honorable. There have to be dozens of families in Azuri that have at least one person still devoted to the Dominion, but it's not lawful to kill them just for that. It's not like they were wearing their prayer belts and chasing us about their fields with pitchforks. They were trying to help us."

Mara opened her mouth to reply, but Amie cut her off. "I'm not saying you're wrong about all of what you said. I'm just saying that what happened wasn't right either." Amie's grip on her sister's arm tightened with insistence. "Can you at least agree that we should go our separate ways? Haven't you had enough of soldiers whether they be of the Dominion or Hzorah? I certainly have."

Mara sighed and shifted the weight of the pack. "Fair enough. We will go our separate ways. But only after we're nearer our home. We don't know who else is out here. There's always the chance that Dominion soldiers found their way out here too. We need protection. We can make it alone once we're within a day of our home."

Mara turned away again and headed to the campfire. Amie stared after her a moment, still burning from the heat of her churning emotions. She wished Mara would actually listen to her, but that wasn't Mara's way. She was beyond headstrong.

Saleh leaned in to nuzzle Amie's neck, and she returned the affection. "We'll be home and away from these awful men soon, Saleh. Then we can show you the best stables

West Hzorah has to offer. Fresh hay, plenty of company, and finally, rest before we have to go to Caldor."

Amie sighed as she petted Saleh's neck. "*If* they let us go at all."

SEVEN

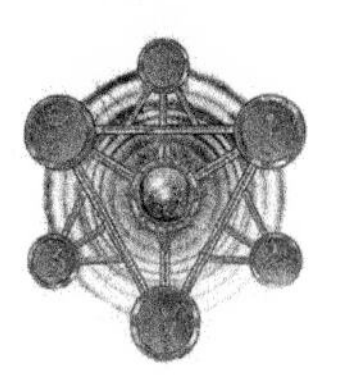

TRAPPED

Mara couldn't believe how fortunate she was. A gentle stream crossed just below her. Barely wide enough to merit a hop, the brook was likely a run-off from the Drunn river. Still, she didn't want to get herself wet and held tight to a network of roots that were exposed after the recent cliffside break. She pulled a small metal needle from her collar and began rubbing it against the dark gray sediment that jutted from the cliff, careful to only stroke it in one direction.

Mara reasoned that the previous night's storm had taken its toll, and lightning had struck the tree at the cliff's edge. The impact broke away some of the land and—in a fortune of all fortunes—magnetized the sediment at the surface.

A smile crossed Mara's lips as she climbed down off of the cliff and turned to her sister's confused stare. She held up the needle. "I have it!"

"A needle?" Amie said dryly. "Congratulations."

Mara's smile broadened. "Thank you. Did you fill the bowl with water?"

"Of course, Your Grace," Amie mocked. "Would you like me to hold the bowl to your lips so that you may have a cool, refreshing drink?"

"Don't jest," Mara said as she pulled a leaf off a tree and crossed to the bowl. "It's unbecoming."

"*You're* unbecoming," Amie muttered, but Mara ignored it. Today was just too lucky to have her sister spoil her mood.

She sat before the bowl and glanced up at the soldiers that stood by the road, talking amongst themselves. It had been a bit too soon for them to stop and rest, but Mara had convinced them that she would faint if they didn't stop at that very moment. It also happened to be the exact moment she'd seen the lodestone.

Mara placed the leaf in the bowl of water then gently balanced the needle on the leaf. When the needle turned in the water and pointed north, she looked back at her sister. "We have a problem."

"I should say so," Amie sighed. "No one is going to drink tea with a needle in it."

Mara's eyes narrowed at her sister. Perhaps she had been too dismissive of her sister's warnings, which had continued periodically over the last few days. Mara had brushed them aside, preferring to act with certainty rather than fear. In response to Mara's hesitance to take her sister's word for it, Amie had become increasingly flippant as the days crawled by.

But now . . . Well, now it was Mara's unpleasant duty to act on certainty.

"It turns out we're going the wrong way," Mara declared. She pointed in the direction of the needle. "That way is north." With her other hand, she pointed again. "That way is west. We've been heading east for at least a day. It has been overcast for the past several days, so that has made it difficult for me to determine if we have been progressing as we should. Now I know that we aren't. We had the good fortune of running into a magnetized lodestone, and I had a needle from the farm."

Amie crouched down to study the needle before she

looked up at her sister. "So where are they taking us? And why?"

"I believe they're trying to take us to Azuri."

Amie pointed at the needle. "Clearly, they aren't."

"Clearly," Mara said. "But what I mean is that *they* believe they are."

Amie raised her eyebrows. "Are you sure?"

"No," Mara said. "But as I said, it has been overcast, and determining direction can be difficult in these conditions without a clear view of the sun or stars."

"And how do we know if this is an accident or not?"

"Simple. We let them know their error."

"But our only advantage is that they don't know that we know."

"True," Mara said. "But they're Hzorah soldiers. They don't have much reason to hurt us as the Dominion soldiers did. It's likely an error, and if they were uncertain, perhaps they felt it embarrassing to admit to a couple of city girls that they weren't entirely sure if they were going the right way."

Amie shook her head. "I don't know."

"Well," Mara said as she got to her feet. "We will momentarily."

Mara crossed back to the road. Amie fell in behind her as the soldiers looked up at her expectantly. Mara flashed a smile the way her father had taught her to do when approaching a patron at the Kruv House. He'd told her that it always disarmed a man to see a pretty girl approaching with a smile and "A man can't possibly think clearly in front of my daughters." Mara had to forcefully push away a torrent of suppressed sorrow as she remembered her father's good advice.

"Are you feeling better?" Normand asked her.

Mara nodded, maintaining her countenance. "I am."

"I have to tell you," Rossok said. "Hanging over a creek

by the root of a tree must be the strangest cure for a headache I've ever seen."

Mara didn't have a response at the ready for that, but Amie was quick to jump in. "It's quite effective. Everyone in *West* Hzorah does it. You must know about it."

Mara turned a warning glare at her sister.

"Well," Rossok said as he shouldered his pack. "We best be off. I want to make good time today."

"About that," Mara said. "I don't think we're going the right way."

"You don't?" Tarub asked, looking to Normand. "Why's that?"

"Well," Mara pointed west. "That way is west, but we've been traveling east for some time now. If we keep in this direction, we'll hit the Great Sea soon."

Tarub and Normand didn't respond. Instead, they looked to Rossok who didn't appear phased at all. "I didn't tell you. We're taking a short detour for supplies. Then we'll be off to Azuri."

Mara shrugged, lifting her own pack slightly. "Between what we received from the farm and the food left out for us by the farmers, we have more than enough to make it back home."

"That's probably true." Rossok nodded. "But Normand here lives in the east. And since we're already headed in that direction, we may as well take him home first."

As if all was settled, Rossok turned and signaled for everyone to follow. Mara shared a look with her sister. Amie's head tilted ever so slightly—a gesture that said: "They're lying."

"Perhaps we should split up," Mara called out.

Rossok, Tarub, and Normand stopped in their tracks and turned back before Rossok answered, "What?"

"We have the supplies we need," Mara said. "There's really no reason for us to continue to slow you down with my constant need for respite."

"It's no bother," Rossok said. "You remind us to take a break. That's good. If it were left up to me, I'd keep my men going until they drop."

Mara smiled again, trying to appear friendly, disarming. "You wouldn't do that. You're a good leader." When Rossok didn't appear to change his mind, Mara said, "But listen. Our inn very much needs us there. Our journey was unplanned, and there are a great many things that we must address. We can't afford to continue east. We must continue on to Azuri."

Rossok sighed as he looked at his comrades. "I can't let you go off on your own. I wouldn't be a good soldier if I let two unarmed and unescorted ladies journey alone. Imagine if word of that got out?"

"I assure you, we won't say a word," Mara said.

Rossok shook his head. "That's really not the point. It's the principal."

"I really must insist that—"

"No."

"What?"

"No."

Mara stared at the man as her smile faded into incredulity. "What do you mean?"

Rossok folded his arms across his chest. "Exactly what I said. I won't allow you to go off on your own. It's not safe. You must go with us."

"You can't force us to—"

"I can, and I am," Rossok said as he let a hand fall to the knife at his belt. "Come on now, before things get messy."

Mara held his gaze for a long moment, but Rossok's hard expression was quite clear. They were going to accompany them whether they liked it or not. Even if she, her sister, and their horse were in the best of conditions, they would have little chance of outrunning or overpowering the three soldiers. They were weaponless, inexperienced in physical altercations, and were not coordinated enough to work together. Pressing the issue was certain to end poorly.

"I see," Mara said, holding her chin high. "Come along, Amie. The soldiers grow weary of waiting for us."

Before Amie could protest, Mara marched onward, falling in line behind the soldiers as they continued down the road toward the eastern horizon. She couldn't allow Amie to exacerbate the situation. The soldiers had now shown their willingness to assault them, and now that the pretense of pleasantry had faltered, the danger was more immediate.

A quick glance at Amie confirmed that she, too, understood the nature of their predicament. But then, it seemed that she had known long before Mara that there was something amiss.

Mara wanted to believe that the soldiers were decent men. She'd given them every opportunity to be what she desperately needed after weeks of relentless chaos and death and hopelessness. She'd clung to every lie and deception, ignored every inconsistency and warning.

All because she wanted—*needed*—it to be true.

But she'd been wrong.

When did I become the naive one?

Amie stared intently at the flames, refusing to even look at her sister. Why couldn't Mara just listen to what Amie had warned her about? Why did she always have to pretend like she knew everything? Why couldn't she just trust her? Even now, Mara sat just a few feet away, calmly eating her bowl of rice as if she hadn't been the one to get them trapped. When Mara casually emptied a small bag of spice into her rice then pocketed the pouch, Amie almost screamed in frustration with her sister's nonchalance.

She could hardly believe it. They were captured *again.* And this time her own sister let it happen.

Somehow, Amie had to get them out of this. She'd gotten lucky with Bam Rav. He'd been the kind of person who had a conscience. The kind of person who, deep down, was looking for an excuse to do the right thing. This Rossok was no such man. He was cunning and manipulative. He lied as easily as . . . Well, as easily as she did. Not that her lies were meant to really hurt anyone. They were good lies.

Amie looked past the fire to where the three men knelt around a quite sizable marble ring that had been carved into the ground—another gift from the people of Hzorah to the soldiers returning home after being relieved of duty. The farm nearby must have had children who thought it would be a fun idea to give some of the soldiers a game to play along with their meal.

Perhaps the other two—Normand and Tarub—would be better targets. Neither appeared to be like Rossok. Just like before, she would have to be patient and wait for her opening. Rossok wouldn't let her near the other two if he thought there was a chance they'd defect.

She hated his confident attitude as if he were entitled to everything he set his eyes on. She hated how he—

Just then, Rossok looked right at her and waved her over.

For a moment, she sat frozen, wondering if she'd been so furious that he'd somehow overheard her very thoughts. It was, of course, ridiculous, so she gathered herself, dropped the half-eaten bowl of rice to the ground, and began to stand.

Mara caught her arm. "Amie, don't—"

Amie pulled away. "Don't what? Don't get close to them? Honestly, Mara, you don't know *everything.*"

Before Mara could respond, Amie hopped to her feet and crossed to the marble circle where the three soldiers sat evenly spaced around the large ring. Not wanting to be close to Rossok, she placed herself between Tarub and Normand, giving herself an appropriate buffer.

"It's uneven," Rossok said. "Thought maybe one of you girls knew how to play."

He said it so casually, with so much familiarity, as if he hadn't just threatened to kill them mere hours before. It sent tingles down her spine, but she forced herself to look at him anyway. "Not anymore. I will play with Tarub. He'll need my help with his shoulder as it is."

Without warning, Rossok tossed a blue shooter in her direction, and Amie caught it out of the air without a moment's hesitation.

Rossok let out a short burst of laughter. "You have a good arm, good reflexes."

"Are you sure you want to play against me?" Amie asked. "You *will* lose."

Rossok's self-assured smile didn't falter. "Please. Show us how you do it in the west."

Amie reveled in the opportunity to show off. She had, after all, warned him. In her younger years, before every boy suddenly became a threat to her virtue and before her father promptly found that he needed much more help at the inn than he could afford to pay, Amie had been quite the marbles champion. She fiercely dominated a marble ring, and though she no longer played, she still kept every shooter she'd won from the boys who thought they had a chance at defeating her.

Just a few more boys who don't know what they're dealing with, Amie thought.

It didn't take long before Rossok and Normand knew *exactly* what they were dealing with. It only took three rounds before they realized that her accuracy wasn't based on luck. And while it was technically against the rules for her to tell Tarub what to do next, she used her body language to suggest how she wanted him to shoot. It wasn't enough to compensate for his lack of skill with his turquoise shooter, but it was enough to set up the ring in a way that played to her advantage.

"You're not bad," Tarub said as Rossok lined up his shot.

"I dearly wish I could say the same for you," Amie said without a hint of humor.

Tarub caught her eye and grinned. "I suppose you're right about that."

Rossok cursed as he missed his shot, and Tarub lined up another strike. This time, Amie didn't have to direct him. The game was so close to won, the last several plays were too obvious to miss. Tarub beamed at her when his shot struck, placing them far enough ahead on the point spread that he and Amie would have to miss the next six turns in order for the other two to catch up. Instead of giving him the approval he clearly wanted, Amie let out a curt "eh."

Tarub sat back before saying in a hushed tone, "You must think we're monsters. This isn't what we wanted—what I wanted."

Amie crossed her arms. "I don't think you're monsters. I think you're men—men who haven't yet found themselves."

"Does anyone really 'find themselves'?"

"Yes," Amie said as she lined up their winning point. "But only if they're truly searching."

She let loose her shooter and with a satisfying crack, nudged her way to another victory.

EIGHT

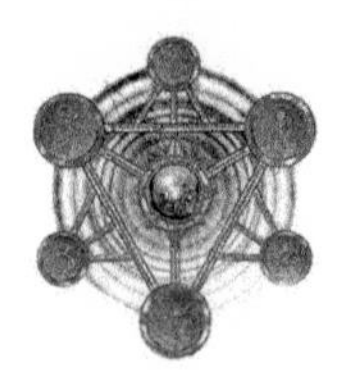

PAYMENT

Amie should have been elated. That's how she always imagined she'd feel when she first set eyes on the Crown City. Far larger in both area and population, the capital of Hzorah was the very mecca of Hzorah culture and trade. Anybody who was somebody either frequented the city often or lived there. Their king and his sons were residents of the city too, and though she didn't have the opportunity to pass close to the Crown Palace, she could see it in the distance, an ever-present fixture against the city's horizon.

No. Instead of absolute rapture, Amie's passions were dulled by fear and uncertainty. She clung to her sister out of requirement rather than comfort, and the three soldiers—for the girls' safety—had encircled them so that the chaos of people that weaved through the streets wouldn't separate their group. Of course, that came with the added and arguably more crucial benefit of keeping the Kruv girls from making their escape. Rossok even managed to guide them through districts infrequently patrolled by the Crown's Guard.

The soldiers didn't break with their facade of chivalry after Mara had confronted them. Tarub, Rossok, and

Normand remained benign, but every suggestion now felt like a well-masked command. The soldiers led the girls through an aging district and toward the city's edge, where large, seafaring vessels lethargically floated near their docks while sailors and soldiers tended to their upkeep and cargo.

Bells of alarm began to toll within. *Could they really be planning to take a voyage?*

Amie wondered why soldiers found her and her sister so alluring that they just *had* to cart them all about the world. She'd never gotten a satisfactory answer out of Bam Rav about why her family had been captured and forced into their journey to the Shadow Peaks. They were simple city girls. They weren't exactly poor, but they weren't the daughters of a lord and had no real political power.

Why us?

A shared glance with her sister confirmed that a trip to the coast was something even Mara hadn't considered. Her sister's transformation from casually disagreeable to keenly focused was subtle, and if Amie hadn't known her sister so well, she may not have noticed it. The soldiers certainly wouldn't. The shift was nearly imperceptible.

Good. At least she's finally paying attention. If she'd only trusted me over these men, we wouldn't be in this mess.

Over the past several days, she'd continued to gently prod Tarub and Normand whenever they'd addressed her without Rossok close enough to hear. She'd started with sympathy. It pained Amie to use her father's death as a mere tool of manipulation, but she knew that Father would forgive her of that. Then, she'd moved into a series of affirmations—at least as many as she could stomach.

"You must feel afraid out here, away from everyone you love in a land you don't know," and *"It must have been awful to have been forced to protect yourselves from those farmers,"* and *"You're trapped, aren't you? You can't go back now, and you'll forever be looking over your shoulders here."*

Usually, they'd fall silent when her comments hit too

close to the questions they were considering themselves, but they managed to keep themselves from giving words to any of their vulnerabilities. Amie could sense their soft spots, but without them speaking them to her, she hadn't quite crossed the threshold of trust she needed to establish.

And now that it appeared the soldiers intended to take them far from home—beyond the borders of their kingdom—time was running short.

The Crown City and its surrounding communities were set on a vast delta that split the city into many islands. Amie's hometown of Azuri bordered the Drunn River. The Crown City was almost a part of it. With so much shoreline, there were many choices for acquiring a sailing vessel, and the soldiers seemed to have intentionally chosen the dingiest sailing community they could find.

When they approached the docks, the sailors that busied themselves with various duties suddenly made themselves scarce while those who remained visible were some of the largest men Amie had ever seen all together in one place. Unphased, Rossok led them right up to one of the largest men on the docks.

"Fine day for sailing," Rossok said with his most endearing smile.

The man before them, his arms folded across his broad chest, grunted in reply. Half a dozen men that cut just as imposing a figure found their way to his side.

Rossok didn't falter. "You know, my grandfather owned a ship. Said that men of the sea were the most resourceful men you could ever meet. Subject to the unpredictable wrath of ocean weather, sickness, long voyages, repairs, and tariffs. Sailors have got to be nimble and quick to see opportunity when they spot it."

The man's demeanor didn't shift. "What do you want, soldier?"

"Well," Rossok said as he glanced back at their party. "You see, we're in a bit of a bind. We need to find our way to the Crehn Isles. And you all look like the right sort to spot an opportunity."

The man continued to glare at Rossok for what felt like an eternity before glancing over his shoulder and making two quick clicks with his tongue. One of the men turned and headed for the drab vessel behind them and returned with another man who wasn't quite as large as his entourage but carried himself with a reasonable amount of authority.

"Well, Tam," the new man said as he approached. "What have we here?"

The bodyguard, Tam, stepped aside to allow the man through. "A few soldiers seem to think they have an 'opportunity' for us, Captain."

"Is that right?" the captain said. "Well, we're quite booked up with *opportunities*. With Caldor preoccupied with snowball fights, business is quite good." He nodded over his shoulder toward the east. "The kind of opportunities you have to offer us belong on a different dock."

"We're on the right dock," Rossok said.

"You are?" The captain let on a smile as he turned to Tam who gave a short shrug. The captain's smile faded away before he turned back to them. "Either you're the stupidest soldiers in all of Hzorah, or you think we're the biggest dolts this side of the city. Take your business elsewhere."

Before the captain could turn away, Rossok made a move, reaching for his waist. The captain's men grabbed hold of him before Rossok could get within inches of his sword, and a fair number of men stepped out of nowhere, pulling daggers as they circled them.

The captain let out a low whistle. "So it's you that's crazy. It's good to know we're not misrepresenting ourselves."

To Amie's surprise, Rossok didn't appear even the least bit concerned. "I don't want to hurt you. You have us all wrong. I was merely moving to remove my uniform."

"I don't think you're our type," the captain said with a grin, and his men laughed.

"Of course not," Rossok said. "I just want to show you what we're really about." He looked to the two men who held him in place. "May I?"

The bodyguards looked to their captain for direction. The captain crossed his arms and cocked his head as he appraised Rossok. "Go on then."

The men released Rossok, but gave him a look that said, "One more sudden move, and it'll be your last."

Rossok slowly untucked and unbuttoned the soldier's coat, careful to not give them any more reason to think he'd do anything foolish. He then slipped his right arm out of his sleeve. The captain and his men leaned in, ever so slightly to see as Rossok tapped his shoulder. Amie and Mara had to crane their heads to see what mark Rossok had that would give him sway over the sailors.

There was none.

The man had to have seen more than twenty-five years, and yet he had no Hzorah Mark.

A chilly realization washed over Amie. These men weren't Hzorah soldiers at all.

"You see," Rossok said. "We don't belong here. But we can't go back to where we came from."

"And where is that?" the captain asked.

"The Crehn Isles."

The captain scratched his chin and looked to the sky. "The Crehn Isles, eh? Now that's a long, long trip. Tam how much did the last man pay that wanted passage to the Isles?"

Tam grunted a laugh. "More than these moppers have, that's for sure."

The captain nodded along and raised fingers as he began to tally the fair. "There was the payment for passage . . . It's a long trip . . . Food, water . . . And then we had to charge more for the location . . . The Crehn Isles isn't the safest place to sail to. The danger of it . . ." He paused and looked at Rossok. "I imagine you have that covered, no?"

"We brought payment," Rossok said.

Tarub and Normand nudged Amie and Mara forward. Amie stumbled but caught her balance. She turned back to the soldiers with wide eyes, but none of them looked to her.

"We have a horse," Rossok said. "It's not in the best condition, but it will be healed in a couple weeks' time. Tall, strong, and not skittish. And these two girls as well. As you said, it's a long voyage. I'm sure your men would like some company to pass the time."

Amie's stomach twisted in knots as she realized what Rossok meant by "company," and a strong impulse to run almost overwhelmed her. Mara took her hand, and Amie clutched her sister's in a tight grip. The captain looked the girls up and down in a way that made Amie's skin want to crawl right off her body. Then he sighed as a small smile took his lips.

This cannot be happening to me. It just can't.

"A generous offer," the captain said. "But my men are hardly in want of their company. They prefer women with experience, and we have bargains with several long-standing establishments. It'd be foolish of us to go back on our word. No deal."

Without another word, the captain turned and the dock resumed its operations as if they weren't there. Amie let out a breath of relief, but her body still trembled with fear and she fought to hold back a sob. Mara give her hand a squeeze of comfort.

"Bring the girls," Rossok snarled as he turned and marched away.

Tarub and Normand took the girls by the shoulders and guided them off the docks and back into the city. Rossok showed no sign of slowing as they pushed through the street traffic and into an empty alley. He turned back to them once they'd sequestered themselves from the public. He paced a step or two before turning and retracing his steps—all that he could manage in the tight alleyway—and Amie cringed as she spotted two rats scurrying away to avoid the sweep of Rossok's booted warpath.

"Well," Normand began, his face dark within the building's shadow. "What do we do?"

Rossok continued pacing as if he hadn't heard the man at all.

"We need more to trade," Tarub said. "Something the sailors actually value."

"But we don't have anything," Normand said. "We could sell the horse, but they didn't seem to think that would be quite enough payment for the voyage."

"We don't have much for supplies."

"We can still sell the supplies we have. Or maybe we can get a discount if we bring our own food and water."

"But that will still cost us."

"Yes, but we might be able to strike a deal with others."

"Perhaps . . . But honestly, I'm starting to think—"

Rossok suddenly stopped his pacing and turned to the two soldiers. "Will you two shut your scorching mouths for two scorching seconds?"

The soldiers quieted, allowing the sound of city traffic and trade to resonate between narrow alley passageways. Men called out their best prices, women chattered and gossiped, oars splashed, cutting through the waters of the city's waterways as the river taxies ferried people about. None of it was as loud as the pulse of fear that drummed in Amie's chest.

His jaw set in resolve, Rossok said, "We kill the girls, cut our losses."

Amie stood in mute shock as the soldier locked eyes with her. Cold and calculating, he held her gaze. Her heart began to race, and every last bit of fight within her surged to the surface, demanding to be summoned to make her very last stand before Desolate's door. Mara's hand clutched hers.

Amie knew that her sister would be ready to fight or run for their lives in the faint hope that the crowded city was enough to hide them away.

But hope of escape was near impossible. They were blocked in by two soldiers in a narrow alley. It would take a stroke of destiny to slip past them, and yet another to outrun the three before they could duck out of sight.

Amie shut her eyes, breaking from Rossok's terrible leer. With every bit of reason she could muster, she pushed aside her instinct to fight the threat head-on. That wasn't the way she'd escaped the last group of soldiers, and considering the circumstances, it certainly wasn't how she would escape this time either.

No, Amie thought. *There's more. There's always another way.*

Her weapon was not the sword. It was the tongue.

Slowly, Amie opened her eyes, again meeting the soldier's icy gaze. "It's a shame, really, that we have to die. We could have made this whole thing so much easier for you."

Almost imperceptibly, Rossok's expression shifted from resolve to uncertainty. "How's that?"

Amie sighed and crossed her arms. "Well, isn't it obvious? We're not country girls. And if you have any bit of wit about you, you'd know that we're not exactly the poorest lot. You targeted us because we look and sound like we have money, that somebody might want us back and be willing to pay for it. You were right."

Rossok grunted. "Little good it did. You're worthless here, and we're not going west."

"We don't have to," Amie said. "We simply take a boat. That's what us *rich* girls do."

"You don't have money," Rossok said. "And if you do, it's too far away to do us any good."

Amie scoffed. "Come now. You can't possibly believe that *gold* is the only way people like us get what they want."

Rossok frowned. "Go on."

"Well, there are times when those of great wealth find themselves in a bind." She held up a hand, as if to weigh their situation. "They need something." She held up the other in counterpoint. "But they don't have gold to afford it at the present. When you have money, you don't just sit on it, you know. It's always being used. What's the point of having money if you're not using it."

Rossok's expression slipped from contemplation to confusion. "Uh huh."

"And so, how do you suppose a situation like that is resolved? Does the rich man simply go without or beg on a street corner? Of course not. Yet, he will acquire what he needs."

Rossok sighed, his confusion giving way to impatience. "What's your point?"

"There is a way that rich girls like us get what we want when we can't pay today," Amie said with a smirk. "It's called credit."

"Credit?" The soldier glanced to the others. "What do you mean?"

As she suspected, the man was clever, but probably never had much money. That meant she knew just enough about money that she could impress him, and he knew too little to question how risky her brewing plan really was.

"If we look the part," Amie said, "there's a fair chance that we can talk our way onto a more reputable ship. You may not be able to get to the Crehn Isles, but you'll probably be able to get to Roanne, and that's a step in the right direction. In fact, you may find that Roanne suits you."

Tarub spoke up from behind. "Look the part?"

Amie nodded as she turned to him. "There are some things we'll need. We don't have much money, so I suggest we get a bit more creative to acquire them. We'll need better clothes, obviously. We'll need to sell our provisions for a little coin. We'll need some to flaunt so it appears that we can make good on our offer—"

"Charcoal!"

Amie turned to look at her sister. "What?"

"Uh . . ." Mara hesitated. "We need charcoal."

Glaring at her sister and hoping she was able to properly communicate how urgent it was that she not interrupt and risk seeding doubt into the soldier's heads, she hissed, "Why do we need charcoal, sister?"

"To filter the water, of course," Mara said, her voice a measure steadier as she straightened in confidence. "We don't want to drink seawater."

Normand cocked his head curiously. "Won't they have their own—"

"I've sailed before," Amie interjected, still unsure why her sister would request something so trivial. "They do have their own filter mechanism, but it's never a fresh or well-maintained system." She met Mara's gaze. "I think it would be wise to have our own."

Mara gave her the slightest of nods.

"We can probably snatch some from a blacksmith," Tarub said, rubbing his chin.

"Alright," Rossok said. "We'll try it the *rich girl* way. But it won't save you if this doesn't work."

Amie gave Rossok her most confident smile. "Then I suppose we'd better get started. I'm in no rush to cross into Desolate."

NINE

ACCOMMODATIONS

Tarub's heart pounded in his chest as he lingered at the market's corner. Unlike Desera's city of Janamah, Eveletia—or the Crown City as it was now called—was far from the stark utilitarianism that the Creed valued. The Crown City's market district sprawled with dozens of clothing shops that rewarded anyone with sufficient coin a variety of fashions.

The men and women who littered the streets casually crossed from outlet to outlet, unaware that their lives were so incredibly indulgent. Tarub couldn't quite grasp what life here would be like. How could so many have so much?

If this is the promised land, Tarub wondered, *why would the Creed want to return here*? The virtues of his doctrine strictly forbid such wastefulness. Hadn't the Creed built this city? How could they not see its perversion?

"There," the girl said from his side. She pointed from the shadows toward the street's end. "Go to that shop there."

Tarub squinted. "The one with the yellow—"

"No, no. Not that one. The one with the blue and the white trim."

Tarub frowned down at her. "Why that one?"

"That's Yarrow's place," Amie said as if it was completely obvious why that shop would be the one he'd need to enter. "There's a girl I know that went there once when she came here. Said it was a bit too easy to steal from, that 'a girl could get the finest for free' there if she was careful."

When Amie met his scowl, he asked, "You're friends with thieves?"

"What makes you think I don't have friends who aren't above thievery?" Amie asked, but relented when he raised his eyebrows. "Fine. I overheard a woman saying so in my father's inn. Happy? You just ruined a perfectly good story."

Tarub turned back to the market and sighed. "How do I know what to get you? We don't exactly have anything like this where I'm from."

"Yarrow's wouldn't have anything out of fashion or season," Amie said.

"You know a lot about this place from second-hand information."

"My aunt has a clothing shop," she said. "I know a lot about a great number of shops and tailors that I've never seen or met."

"Right."

"Well," Amie said. "Go on then. The longer you stand here, the harder it'll be to work up the courage to do what you *must*."

Tarub stumbled forward when Amie gave him a gentle but firm shove. He turned a sharp glare back at her, but she shooed him onward. The plan was simple. He'd enter the shop and begin to "shop around" as the girl put it, and then she'd distract the shopkeep while he stuffed his pack with the clothes they needed. A simple plan with a simple objective.

Still, Tarub wished he was with Rossok and Mara, and that Normand had to do the clothes shopping. Bartering their supplies away felt more like something he'd be competent at—something he could do relatively guilt-free. But then, he was certain Rossok would turn the matter into dishonest work somehow. And there was the charcoal they needed for fresh water that they'd have to steal. So, either way, he'd be getting his hands dirty.

He'd been doing that a lot these past several days. Every day, Hzorah continued to shift from promised land to hellscape, its fertile grounds the seedbed for his darkest impulses. Tarub managed to compartmentalize what he was doing as a means to an ultimately good end, but now that the sisters knew what they were doing, he found it increasingly difficult to keep his conscience at bay.

But it was almost done now. If this went as planned, they'd be off to Roanne and then perhaps the Crehn Isles and free to live their lives as they saw fit. It wasn't exactly as he envisioned it, but that was the only hope he had to keep him pushing onward.

As he entered Yarrow's and delivered the lines Amie had coached him on just several minutes prior, the young and sharply dressed shopkeep barely took his gaze from his pen and parchment at the shop's tailoring bench. He couldn't have seen more than fifteen years.

Would it really be this easy?

Amie entered just a moment later and gave a similar speech, but didn't give any clue that she knew Tarub. She crossed to a wall that displayed several pre-cut outfits. When he caught her eye, she looked to the clothing at her feet and gave him a slight nod before picking up the dress just in front of her and walking it to the tailor's bench.

"I don't have much time to shop today," she said to the boy. "I'd love to see what this looks like. May I try it on?"

The boy looked her up and down. "I—" He cleared his throat and blinked. "My mother usually—"

Before he could finish, Amie reached out and took his hand. "Don't be overly modest. I won't strip down in front of you. I just need your help with the back buttons."

As she pulled the boy to his feet and guided him to the

partition at the shop's rear corner, she looked back at him over her shoulder to give him a coquettish smile, and in the same motion, caught Tarub's eye with an expression that he could almost hear—*this is your chance.*

"Don't dally. I really am in a rush!" With a sharp motion, Amie pulled the boy behind the partition.

Tarub turned and stuffed the two light blue dresses that Amie had pointed out into his pack. He then crossed the store to where they kept men's outfits. The Hzorah army's uniforms didn't match the story they'd concocted.

"The buttons down the back are too hard to reach. Don't be shy. Have you never touched a woman before?"

Tarub scanned a line of servant livery. There was nothing of the sort in Desera, but he figured anything bleached stark white wouldn't suit a bodyguard. He decided to go with the outfits that most closely resembled that of a soldier: a dark gray—nearly black—uniform with golden buttons, a red sash, and a simple but sturdy belt that accommodated a sword and dagger.

"I think I'm just a touch too short for this dress. The hem touches the floor. If only it was taken up to here . . . Quickly, hold it here and here at my hips so I can see what it looks like taken in. Hold it firm!"

Tarub stuffed the uniforms into his pack and hoped that he'd judged the proportions of Rossok and Normand correctly. Filled to the brim and overflowing, he had to press down on the clothing to force it into his pack so that it would buckle shut. If he, his friends, and these girls were willing to steal from the unsuspecting, he should expect that there might be others who'd try the same thing if given an easy opportunity.

"Well, that's disappointing," Amie said, her tone set with conclusion. "I was sure this would be the one. I suppose you should allow me to undress again—no, wait! The buttons. I can't reach remember?"

Tarub hastened to exit the shop before the boy came

back from behind the partition and made sure to open and close the shop's door gently to avoid alerting the shopkeep. He exhaled in the open air as though he'd been holding his breath for an hour. He hugged the pack close as he waited for Amie to exit the shop.

The door opened not long after, and Amie waved a final goodbye to the boy inside. "Of course I'll be back. You're the most helpful shopkeep I've ever met!" She shut the door behind her and turned to him. "You've gotten what we need?"

Tarub nodded. "Yes. Let's go before he realizes there's anything missing."

With a hand on her shoulder to ensure they didn't separate, Tarub guided Amie through packed throngs of city pedestrians and to the east where they'd agreed to meet under a tall, white tower visible from nearly any point in the city. Thankful the city wasn't like Janamah—nearly flat except for the Shrine of the Creed—he followed the streets as they wound against the curve of the city's canals or crossed them with arching, stone-worked bridges. As long as he kept the pearl tower in view, he was able to make steady progress toward their destination.

"Is this how you envisioned it?" Amie asked as they reached the apex of a bridge that framed the distant Hzorah Palace as a brush of splendor below an evening sun.

"I suppose I don't know what I expected the city to look like."

"Not the city," Amie said. "Killing farmers, stealing from shops, sailing to a far-off land . . . Is that what you hoped for when you left the Dominion army?"

Tarub's jaw set tight as he guided the girl back onto a narrow street against a tall wall of stone worked buildings. "No."

"What did you expect?" Amie asked. "What was your dream?" When Tarub grunted dismissively, Amie pressed on. "There's another way, you know."

"We are trying the other way," Tarub said. "You suggested it."

"Yes," Amie said as a bend along the waterway brought the white tower before them. "But there's no reason why we have to go with you once you're on board. You don't need us anymore. We can just be on our way."

"I'm not a fool," Tarub said. "You'd report us. The ship would be boarded and searched, and our heads would be on a pike before the day's end."

"That's not true."

"It's not? Tell me then how things will proceed."

"Well," Amie said and then turned about to face him. She continued backward as the street broadened to accommodate a courtyard filled with budding summer flowers that swayed in the gentle breeze, waiting for their moment in the sun. "First of all, we have little reason to report someone who escorted us from such a far-flung region. We have a life to get back to, and the testimony alone would take up too much of our time. You want out. We want out. Simple."

Amongst the tower's lush gardens were benches for the public's enjoyment. The white structure appeared to be a monument of some sort, no doubt dedicated to some wicked Hzorah ideal. He sat with Amie and considered her words. Rossok was right. There was no way they could risk letting the girls go, but Amie's original question gnawed at the core of him.

Is this what I expected? Is this what I dreamed my new life to be?

Since he, Rossok, and Normand had escaped from the Creed's army, none of it had gone the way he'd thought it would. He'd help kill three men on a farm, kidnapped two girls, and was now stealing clothes and supplies before he cheated his way into a free voyage to another unknown land.

It was their fault, a part of him whispered. If those farmers had never pried into their business, they'd still be alive. If this girl's sister hadn't taken it upon herself to question their path, they wouldn't be captives. If those sailors had simply given them the time of day. . . .

But then . . . Perhaps if they'd actually listened to the farmers, they may not have killed them, may not have turned them in. Maybe they could have worked and earned their keep on the farm. Maybe they could have found community there, built an honest life the way they'd intended to all along. At least the way he'd intended to.

All the girls had wanted was to go home, but Rossok had convinced him that tagging along with the girls would benefit them. In a way, they were captives from the very start. If they'd let them go when they were first found out, they could have made their way without all this trouble. There couldn't have been a place to report them for dozens of miles, and by that time, they would have been too far gone to be caught.

And now that he truly considered it, those sailors would have been scorching fools to even entertain taking them up on their offer.

He looked into Amie's eyes as she watched him intently. There had been so many opportunities for them to change their course for the better, but they were lost now. There was no turning back.

"It's not that simple," Tarub said. "Perhaps when we get to Roanne—"

"You'll change?" Amie cut in. "You'll stop following every Desolate-bound order Rossok gives you? Honestly, Tarub, look at yourself. Why do you follow that man? Why does *either* of you? He's nasty and hateful and . . . and . . ."

"A bastard."

"Well," Amie said as she looked to a passing couple that strolled by, hand in hand. "A lady doesn't use such a word but yes. He's a looger bastard."

Before he knew it, Amie took his hand and held it tight. "Don't let him define you. Don't let violence be who you are. You almost died from that arrow, but you have a second chance now. Do you really want to waste that? Don't—"

A forced laugh sounded from behind them. Tarub pulled his hand away and jumped to his feet. Behind them Rossok, Normand, and Mara strolled forth. Tarub stepped away from Amie, and a grin spread across Rossok's face. Relieved of the remainder of their supplies, the horse, weapons, and the soldier uniforms, all that remained was a coin purse that Rossok held close to his chest.

"Tarub, Tarub, Tarub," Rossok mocked. "I didn't know you were one for the blondes. Didn't you say your sweetheart had hair as black as nightfall?"

Tarub opened his mouth to protest as the full wrath of Amie's sister's iron gaze arrested him. "We were talking. That's all."

As Amie stood, Mara swept in to stand between them. "See to it that that's all you do."

Rossok's grin widened, and he clapped Tarub on the back. "You dog! I knew I loved you for some reason. Just wait. When we get to the Crehn Isles, I'll need a right-hand man for the ladies."

His face burning, Tarub tried to pull away, but Rossok didn't relent. "We made out with a healthy sum. I don't like being without my sword but I kept one of the knives in case of trouble." With a pat to his sidearm, he gave cruel look to Amie. "Alright, girl. It's time. Don't think to turn the tables on us when we get there. I'm quick with a blade, and you and your sister will die before the words are half out your mouth."

Seemingly unphased by Rossok's remarks. Amie turned on her heel and led the party back to the docks.

If there was a harsher contrast between the location of the previous shipyard and the one they now approached, Tarub couldn't imagine it. While the previous docks had been lined with vessels of various size and grandeur, none of them could begin to rival the comparative luxury that these docks offered. Still dominated by trading vessels, the docks were well-maintained, and the shiphands were far less covert in what they hauled on and off of their ships.

Amie, as confident in her approach of a large transport vessel as she was with the clothing shop, strolled right up to a man who sat at a dock-side desk with pen and parchment at hand, scribbling away as another sailor dictated an assorted list of figures.

Tarub tugged at the collar of his new clothing. He'd never worn anything so formal, and there was little room for breathing in the outfit he'd chosen for them. The sisters, however, wore their dresses with elegance. *If I didn't know any better, I'd think they were actually from a great Hzorah house.* Tarub didn't know firsthand what that would look like, but the way Amie now carried herself, she could be wearing a spud sack, and he'd think her royal.

Amie stopped before the desk, but didn't bother to vie for their attention. Instead, she stood still and expectant, as if her very presence was enough for them to drop everything they were doing to attend to her needs. Wonder of wonders, it only took a moment before the dock manager paused his work to address her.

"Uh . . . Can I help you, Miss . . ."

"Lady Kruv," Amie said. "I expect that your vessel is to depart within the hour?"

"An hour, perhaps two, Lady Kruv."

"Very good," Amie said. "This is my sister. She's my elder but mute, so I speak for her. And the three behind us are our personal escorts. I expect you have our quarters prepared?"

The man looked back to his notes, scanning. "I'm sorry,

Lady Kruv, but I have no record of your reservation. Perhaps you have the wrong vessel?"

"That Desolate-bound dolt!" Amie hissed before turning to Mara. "I've told Father to be done with that runner of his. He can't even accomplish the simplest task." Mara, now stuck within her role as the mute, only raised her brow in response. Amie turned back to the man. "It is absolutely imperative that we be on this vessel. My Father is a new Low Lord—Lord Kruv, you've heard of him, no?"

"Uh. I'm not—"

"High Lord Bendeth has given his explicit instruction that we oversee the establishment of a new erida stock out of Roanne. Good drink for the High Lord has been quite a burden, and my father's reputation as a prominent innkeeper has won us this important task. The Kruv House in Azuri. You've heard of it, yes?"

"Yes, my Lady, but I—"

"Of course," Amie said with a smile. "Everyone has. Were it not for the fact that our very status is at jeopardy, I'd take the time to wring that runner's neck before I sent him packing, but Lord Bendeth wouldn't find that a suitable excuse to postpone our departure."

"Of course not, my Lady."

Amie held out her hand to her side, and when nothing appeared in it, she turned a glare to Rossok. Taking the hint, Rossok dropped the purse into her hand.

"We only came with enough to take care of our expenses while in Roanne. That fool runner . . . But I can offer you a measure now and another measure when we arrive. You may credit the remainder to High Lord Bendeth's account. We couldn't ask you to take us on without *something* in your hand right now, now could we?"

"That's not—"

"Of course it's necessary," Amie said as she slid two silver marks across the table then reached in for a third.

"And this one is for your trouble. We have been quite the inconvenience."

Tarub had no idea if the sum Amie had placed before the man was reasonable—his station in life was rigid due to the Creed's lack of interest in a wasteful system of monetary exchange—but the man only hesitated a moment before taking the coin. After thumbing through the parchment on his desk, the man appeared to reach a conclusion.

"We have a grain storeroom that we can fit you in," The man said, as he looked up from his parchment. "It's no place for a lady, but all other quarters have been paid for by—"

"That will do," Amie said.

"There won't be much for accommodations. And there's the risk of rats."

Though Amie did visibly flinch at the mention of rodents, she didn't relent. "We will make it work."

"And you'll all have to—"

"When you've made the sale," Amie said, cutting him off, "don't undermine yourself by giving the passenger more reason to reconsider." She glanced back at Tarub and gave him a slight nod. "Bring our packs. This sailor will show us our lodgings."

Before anyone else could say a word, Amie started off toward the ship, forcing the tallyman to send a sailor jogging to catch up with them.

Up a short stairway and onto the ship's deck and they stepped onto the boat. Normand caught Tarub's eye with a look of disbelief that they'd actually talked their way onto a ship. Sure, they'd given the man money, but Tarub had a feeling they'd severely underpaid for the service.

The ship's crewman led them across the busy ship deck and down a railed ladder where a broad storeroom lead to a narrow corridor. Their footfalls heavy against the dusty hardwood, they stopped at the aft end of the ship before a narrow door.

"It's not much," the sailor said as he opened the door to

reveal a cramped closet of a room with the stale air of grain and ale. "Stay below deck until it's safe, we have strict rules about passengers roaming about. Too many have lost their wits when they're out on the water and attempt to jump ship. I suggest taking deep breaths. We won't hesitate to lock you in the brig. I'll bring blankets after we set sail. There's a meal bell. You'll go to the larger storeroom to get it. We don't have a designated meal hall, and we don't eat with our passengers besides. If you get sick, find your way to the privy just off the large storeroom back yonder. . . ."

The party waited patiently as the soldier prattled on, explaining all they'd need to know about the ship, their destination, who to talk to if there's trouble, and what's expected of them if there's the misfortune of severe weather, an encounter with a leviathan—whatever that was—or a pirate raid. The sailor made it sound as if the risks were low, but now that Tarub had heard it all plain, he wasn't sure if taking a ship was actually a safe plan.

Eventually, the sailor left them to the room, and the five of them crammed into the tight confines. There was just enough floor space for them to sit or lie. Chairless, bedless, and a lone candle to illuminate the enclosure, Normand set to arranging sacks of grain to accommodate a more comfortable journey, and Tarub bent to the task of helping him.

"Well," Mara said, her arms crossed as she stared intently at Rossok. "You have what you want. We have no business at all in Roanne. You don't need us anymore. Let us go. You've already set us back far enough."

Matching her posture, Rossok crossed his arms. "No."

"Why not?" Mara protested. "What could you possibly gain from us in a land we aren't familiar with?"

Tarub paused to look at Rossok. "Rossok, maybe she's right. We've put them through enough and—"

"I said no, scorch it!" Rossok turned an enraged glare to Tarub that stopped him mid-sentence. "If we let them off this ship, they'll go right to the port guard. The port guard will force their way onto the ship and arrest us."

Mara threw her arms in the air. "Are you serious? Are you *that* paranoid?"

"There's a world of difference between paranoid and precisely cautious, dear girl." Rossok sneered. "Perhaps you should take a lesson from me so that you don't get caught up with men you can't handle next time."

Mara didn't back down. Instead, she leveled an intense frown at Rossok. "Yes. Perhaps I should."

"There must be some other way," Amie piped in.

"The safest way for us all to part is for us to slit your pretty throats," Rossok concluded as he plopped down on a sack of grain just as Normand placed it behind him. "But that'd leave too much of a mess, and then we'd have to contend with the sailors. And I don't think you'd prefer that end over one where you keep your lives."

Amie nodded. "So, what's the alternative?"

Rossok leaned back, making himself comfortable. "We keep playing the part until we reach our destination. Once we get to Roanne, we'll be done with each other."

Tarub watched as the sisters shared a look. He hated that this had gotten so messy. He never would have imagined that their situation would have escalated to this point. He didn't like it, and he was the one with the advantage. He couldn't fathom how these two girls were taking it.

If it came to it, he didn't want to kill them. They'd done nothing to wrong them. If anything, they were a tremendous aid to their efforts.

No. If it came to it, he wouldn't hurt them. And he wouldn't let Rossok hurt them either. They didn't deserve that.

"So, what's it gonna be?" Rossok asked, closing his eyes as if the matter was already decided. "A pleasant sail across the sea or your untimely death?"

TEN

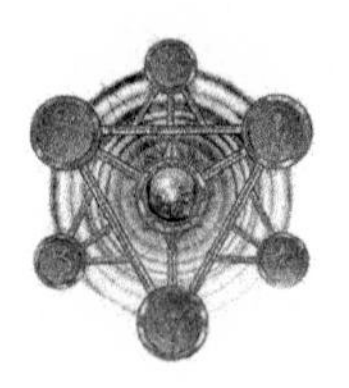

A WELL-EXECUTED PLAN

It hadn't really been much of a choice. The smallest glance from Mara confirmed for Amie that they were going to take their chances on staying alive and continuing on to Roanne. After that, the room had fallen into a drab silence with only distant gulls squawking over the gentle pulse of the sea against the ship's hull.

Amie tried to relax and she sunk deep into the sack of rice that cushioned her bottom from the hard, wooden floor. She supposed that she should be grateful. At least they weren't dead. At least she'd gotten to finally see the Crown City. At least she was on an adventure, awful as it was.

Honestly, Amie thought. *Adventures are not supposed to be this grim*. If she ever saw another bard she'd have a word with them about the way they sold adventure to tavern patrons.

Against her better judgment, the tug of exhaustion stole past her defenses. She had just slipped into a wisp of a dream that may have been about blistered feet and stolen dresses when an insistent tap on her arm brought her back to reality.

A bell sounded in the distance, and Amie could just barely make out the call of a sailor that announced their departure. She glanced to Mara—whom Amie assumed woke her—as she slowly stood and stretched with nonchalance. Rossok straightened as he watched Mara turn back to Amie and extend her hand. Unsure what her sister was up to, she took it and allowed Mara to assist her to her feet.

"I need to use the privy," Mara said. "I'm afraid that the ship's rocking has done something awful to my bowels." She looked at Amie. "I think I need some assistance."

Rossok's face scrunched in disgust before he waved her on. "Go on. But if you take longer than I expect you should, we're coming to check. And they won't let you above deck to jump overboard. We've set sail and they—"

"I know," Mara said. "That's why I waited until after we set sail. I'd prefer to do this without supervision. My sister's involvement is embarrassment enough."

Rossok grunted and rolled over in his makeshift pallet. "Be quick about it."

Amie followed Mara out of the small storeroom and had to walk briskly to keep pace with her sister's determined march. The sea was calm this close to the port, and on a ship this size, a walk down the narrow corridor below deck was not as unsteady as Amie had worried it would be. After crossing into the large, open storeroom and winding their way through an assortment of goods, Mara paused near the stairs that lead up to the ship's deck and took hold of her sister's arm.

"Stay right here," Mara said. "Keep watch."

"Watch? Why don't we just try to jump overboard or at least tell someone about our situation?"

But Mara had already turned and slipped away, continuing to mill through the supplies and occasionally lifting a tarp or opening a set of crates. "And risk being locked in the brig for hysterics? No. Then we'll be trapped for sure."

Amie let it go on for a minute or so before her lack of patience met her abundant curiosity. She crossed her arms and let out an exaggerated sigh. "So, are you going to tell me what you're looking for or are you going to do your usual

'Mara act' where I look like a dolt while you get to smugly fill me in on the details of your half-baked plans?"

"Smug?" Mara asked, then with greater incredulity, "Half-baked?"

"It's like you don't even hear yourself when you speak."

"Perhaps if you weren't always yapping away, I'd —Aha!"

Amie craned to see what her sister had discovered. Mara appeared from behind a large, wooden crate with a hollow metal pipe and a grin plastered across her decidedly smug face. She waved Amie over and began leading them both back down the corridor.

"Really," Amie scoffed as she caught up to her. "Your plan is to bludgeon them to death? Even if we somehow manage to take on all three, how are we supposed to hide their bodies? Neither of us is particularly strong, and it'd completely blow our cover if they discover we'd hurt the very people we employ."

"Don't be so simple, Amie. I know that I can't win a battle of brute strength," Mara said. "I'll take care of the escape, but I need you to get them out of the room." As they approached the storeroom door, she turned back to Amie and lowered her voice. "Can you do that?"

"Why—"

"I'm not as good at talking my way out of situations," Mara whispered. "I admit that you're brilliant at it. It's unsettling how good you are at it, but in our current state, I'm appreciative."

Amie's mouth nearly dropped open. "Is that a compliment?"

"Can you do it?"

"Yes."

"Good," Mara said before turning and opening the door.

Mara stepped through the door, trying to make the fact that she now carried a metal pipe to be the most natural thing in the world for her to return with. As she expected, the Dominion soldiers' attention was aroused at their return. Though they didn't tackle her, she could tell that the pipe presented enough of a threat that their muscles were tense with anticipation.

Slowly, Rossok stood. "What's the pipe for?"

With a soft clink, Mara let the pipe's end slip to the floor. "This? It's for water filtration. Remember? It's best if we don't trust the water."

"Where'd you get it?" Normand asked.

The question was a bit unexpected, but while Mara hesitated, Amie was quick to fill in the details. "We requested it from one of the sailors who came below deck. They were as perplexed as you and assured us that the water they filtered was fine to drink, but we insisted our good health was vital—that the stomach of a city girl can be quite delicate."

When Rossok looked to Tarub and Normand, Amie gave a dramatic sigh. "Did you really think we'd try to bludgeon you to death? We're not *that* stupid. Give us a bit of credit."

No one should be able to lie this easily, Mara thought, but as a bit of tension left Rossok's shoulders, Mara silently thanked her sister for being too mischievous for her own good.

"When people feel trapped," Rossok said, "they get desperate. You can't blame me for thinking you'd go and do something crazy."

Amie shrugged. "Speaking of desperate, after the sailors brought back a pipe—which I assume required the captain's approval—the sailors told us to send for you three to bring down the food for the first leg of our journey."

"Why didn't they just give it to you?" Rossok asked.

Amie managed to look taken aback. "We're ladies, Rossok. It wouldn't be proper. And it's likely far too heavy."

"I don't know how you feel," Normand said, "but I'm half-starved. Let's bring it down now before they decide we don't need as much as they've rationed us."

Tarub stood to leave with them, but Rossok held up a hand. "No, Tarub. Someone needs to stay here with the girls. We can't leave them alone." Tarub only shrugged before leaning back against the room's wall.

"By all means," Amie said. "Doesn't much matter to me how we get the food down here. As long as we do."

Mara breathed again as Rossok and Normand stepped out of the room. Amie's plan had worked. Almost. It wouldn't take long before Rossok and Normand discovered that there was no such interaction between them and the crew. And even if it went smoothly, they couldn't enact Mara's plan with Rossok watching them.

"Whoa!" Tarub cried out and held up a hand. "What are you doing?"

Mara turned to see Amie with her dress halfway over her head, exposing far more than what was decent.

"I'm changing back into our travel clothes," Amie said. "I want to eat in something comfortable, something I don't have to worry about staining."

Quickly, Mara nodded her agreement. "That's an excellent idea!" And she reluctantly began the process of undressing.

"But I'm right here!" Tarub said, his hands shielding his face as though the sun had appeared within the tiny storeroom.

"Then by all means, Tarub," Amie said. "Step out for a moment."

Tarub edged himself to the room's door, his eyes still averted. "I'll be just outside the door, so don't try anything."

"Of course," Amie said in as earnest a voice as Mara had ever heard.

As soon as Tarub shut the door behind him, Mara finished removing her dress and emptied her pockets. Everything was in place. She smiled in what she decided wasn't smug but well-deserved appreciation for a well-executed plan.

"I hope whatever you're planning works. They won't be gone long, and I don't think we'll be able to—" Amie paused as she looked at what Mara had dumped onto the wooden floor. "What are those for?"

Mara lifted each one by one. "Niter, charcoal, and . . ." She held up the last item. "And this is sulfur powder. Found it in the storeroom along with the pipe. They use it to help keep rats away, preventing them from infesting the grain stores."

Amie gripped his sister's arm. "Mara! Are you telling me we don't have rats on this boat? That's wonderful news! And here I thought the trip was going to be abysmal because of the rats. Now we can enjoy it!"

Mara frowned at Amie's deep sarcasm. "Your humor is unbecoming, Amie."

"*You're* unbe—"

"What's important," Mara interrupted as she produced the bowl she'd used to make her compass, "is what I can do with these ingredients." She pulled a long line of thread from her dress and handed it to her sister. "Take this and break it into six equal parts."

"Why?"

"Just do it! We don't have much time."

Mara leaned into the work, quickly mixing her ingredients in the correct proportion. Then, she placed a generous scoop into the six small bags the farmers had left at the rest stops to spice their meals.

"Here," Amie said, holding out what were not entirely equal sections of thread. "What now?"

"Hold the pipe steady here, horizontally."

Amie did as Mara instructed while Mara tied off each

bag, leaving a short lead of thread. She then retrieved the six marbles she'd salvaged from the marble pit and stuffed one of them and a small sack of powder into the pipe's end.

"We're going to use the candle on the wall to light this end here," Mara said and pointed to the thread. "It's called a fuse. The threads in our dresses are cotton. They'll burn easily and quickly." She pointed to the room's wall. "I'll point the end of the pipe here. When it finishes burning, there will be an explosion. It'll blast a hole in the wall. We'll set off all six charges. If distributed correctly, they should weaken the integrity of the ship's hull enough for us to break through."

Amie stared at Mara with wide eyes. "Where in Desolate did this idea come from? How do you even know how to do this?"

"Amie," Mara said. "Gavini and I have so much to teach you, but we'll never have the opportunity if we don't make our way to Caldor." When Amie slowly nodded, Mara approached the candle. "Bar the door as best you can. This will be loud, and Tarub will want to investigate."

When her sister was clear of the pipe, Mara used the room's candle to light the fuse. As she expected, the thread burned quickly, and she redoubled her grip on the pipe, preparing for a strong recoil.

Mara had been prepared for the recoil, and she held it the pipe firm. What she hadn't expected was the deafening pop as the marble burst from the hollow shaft. But she didn't let the unexpected volume keep her from continuing to execute her plan. It was now or never.

Quickly, she reloaded the pipe with the second round, lit the fuse, and aimed. The sound no longer surprising, she watched as the projectile plunged through the boat's hull with such tremendous speed, she couldn't even track it with her eyes.

"Mara . . ."

While she reloaded, Mara turned to her sister who

leaned with all her weight against the door. Tarub was shouting now and rattling the door, and Mara knew that he'd break through when he put his full effort into getting into the room. Amie had very little chance of keeping him out for very long.

"Four more shots to go," Mara said. "Keep him outside."

Before Amie could retort, the third round went off, then a fourth. The pungent odor of hot powder filled the room. The pipe's smoke churned, illuminated by beams of sunlight, of freedom.

By the time Mara had loaded the fifth round, Tarub began to slam himself against the door, and Amie was only just managing to slam it back shut against his intrusion. But just as she had the final round loaded, Amie and Tarub both fell into the room, her sister just barely managing to escape the fall of the door and Dominion soldier as they crashed to the floor. Recovering quickly, Tarub leapt to his feet just as Mara backed away from him, edging back to the candle to light the final fuse.

Tarub held out and hand. "What's going on in here? What are you doing? What is that?" His questions cascaded in quick succession, his confusion mounting as he took in the scene.

Before Tarub had the opportunity to stop her, Mara lit the final fuse and shot Tarub a warning look. "Move out of the way or you'll get seriously injured!"

"What—"

One last deafening crack sent the final marble through the hull, just barely missing Tarub, and making the sixth and final break point in the ship's hull.

"Stop it!" Tarub shouted and grabbed Amie's arm to restrain her.

"Tarub, we have to escape," Amie pleaded with the soldier. "We can't go to the Crehn Isles."

Mara turned as several of the ship's crewmen nearly fell

down the stairs from the deck and stared in disbelief down the hall. Their time had run out. Quickly, she turned and snatched up their packs.

"You can come with us," Amie told Tarub. "We can help you find a new home. But you can't start fresh if you keep following Rossok!"

Mara pushed Amie's pack into her arms. "We have to go!"

Amie took the pack but didn't break eye contact with Tarub. "What do you say? Start over with us? Be free of the Dominion forever?"

There was a moment of hesitation before Tarub shook his head. "I can't stay here. I wouldn't be accepted. I have to continue on."

"Then at least let us go," Mara said. "Do you truly want us to suffer with you? Do you want us to die like those farmers?"

"Tarub," Amie said, "It's never too late to do the right thing. Never."

With a sigh, Tarub again shook his head then sighed. He let go of Amie before stepping aside.

"It's time," Mara said to Amie. "This is going to hurt, but we'll need to break down the wall."

"How?" Amie asked.

"The same way Tarub broke down the door. It's weak now."

For once, Amie didn't argue, but the sailors who'd made their way down the hall *did* protest. Tarub stepped between the crew and the girls, and Mara gave Amie a quick nod as she shouldered her pack

"One, two, three!"

Together Mara and Amie threw themselves at the wall, eyes closed against the splintering wood. They burst into the open air and then down into the sea's depths.

ELEVEN

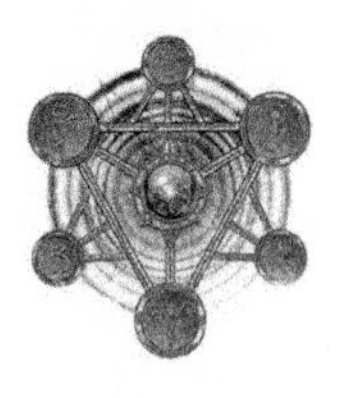

SCIENTIA

Tarub leaned against the hole in the ship's side, watching Amie and Mara swim to shore. At first, he was worried. There wasn't water for swimming where he'd been raised, and he doubted he'd be able to keep his head above water, but the sisters made it look easy.

Soon, he was pulled away from the breach and pinned against the wall. Sailors shouted at him, demanding that he explain what happened, and cursing more relatives than possible for a man to have. Rossok and Normand stumbled into the room, followed by another man who appeared to be the vessel's captain. They, too, were forced into the same corner as Tarub.

The captain set to ordering the crew to start repairs rather than return to dock before his fury turned on the three of them.

"What did you do to my scorching ship, you bloody moppers?"

Rossok and Normand immediately looked at Tarub, and Tarub shook his head, not even knowing where to begin. Half of him couldn't begin to answer his question. The other half was in such awe that he'd seen what he'd seen that words failed him.

"It was . . ." Tarub began, trying to reason it out. "It was magic!"

"Magic?" The captain's fury didn't diminish, but he somehow made room for confusion. "What do you bloody mean magic?"

"They had a stick that shot fire." Tarub pointed. "The fire made a hole in the ship!"

"If that's not the most ridiculous scorching story . . ."

The captain went on, but Tarub had already stopped listening. Was that really magic? He didn't know much about magic. All he knew was that Titan would return, and with it, so would magic. Had he just witnessed the return of magic? What else could explain what he'd just witnessed?

Magic or not, those girls were something different, something special.

Perhaps Titan's blessings were with them too, Tarub thought. Perhaps they weren't the heathens he was taught that they were.

It didn't take long before the sailors bound and ushered them to what appeared to be the ship's brig. Apparently, the captain preferred to continue the voyage rather than turn back.

"What will they do with us?" Normand said to neither of them in particular.

Rossok grunted. "I don't know. Sell us for slaves? Toss us overboard when they get good and ready?"

"What do we do?" Normand asked, his voice unsteady.

"I suggest," Rossok said before turning away from them, "shutting your mouth so I can get some sleep."

Drenched and freezing, Amie held herself close as she shuffled down the street in soggy leather shoes. Her arms ached. She couldn't remember ever swimming so desperately for so long. And for a time, she feared that the shore was too far away to reach. Something inside her, though, wouldn't let her stop, wouldn't let her sink. Stroke after stroke, she'd fought until the shore was nearly within reach and only the violent pull of the undertow stood between her and safety.

There had been an audience to witness their arrival. Mara's contraption had been loud enough that it was heard across the docks, but Mara ignored the questions as she set one unsteady foot before the other and persisted into the anonymity of the Crown City's foot traffic.

"I'm afraid to ask," Amie finally said as they took to a bridge over a narrow canal, "how you did what you did, but I will. What was that? Was that . . . was that magic?"

Mara snorted a short laugh as she tucked wet hair back behind her ears. "Magic? No. There is no one who can actually perform magic, not without that magic having been originally orchestrated with the assistance of Wizard Titan."

Unconvinced, Amie pressed on. "That's not magic? *That's* not magic? What do you call it then?"

"Scientia."

"What?"

Mara looked her in the eye. "Remember how I said that there was much that Gavini and I needed to teach you?" When Amie nodded, she went on. "Magic is simply power —raw, untamed, unfocused. But what we think of as magic is far from unnatural. It's just as real and natural as the ground beneath your feet, the water dripping from your hair, the sun's warmth on your skin. It's where Desolate and Continua meet—the very universe unlocked."

There had always been something that Gavini worked on in his relative isolation outside of Azuri. When her father allowed her and Mara to visit the man, he'd taught her to read, to think, to yearn for more than the comforts a life working at her father's inn would offer. The things he went on to teach Mara were of little interest to Amie, and Gavini had respected that. Amie would tag along and spend much of her time there cooking or reading a number of books he'd kept, filled with stories. But even with the time they'd been there together, she'd never seen Gavini teach Mara anything like she'd seen on that ship.

Amie's eyes widened as realization crested in her mind. "You used to sneak away at night?"

Again, Mara looked at her sister. "Yes."

"The one time I snuck away to help Tele—"

"The one time?" Mara asked. "Amie, you used to go out at night *all* the time. I believe you did it more often than I."

Amie looked straight ahead, her cheeks flushing. "How'd you know?"

"I knew it," Mara said. "Father knew too."

With a jerk, Amie turned back to her sister. "He knew?"

Mara nodded. "Father knew that keeping you in the inn too much would make you resentful. He allowed you to go off at times just to give you a breath of freedom."

"And he did the same for you?"

"No," Mara said. "I was *actually* good at hiding it."

Mara stopped suddenly and scanned the stone wall of a smithy. She reached out and took hold of a stone just above eye level. After a few tugs, the stone came free. She set the rock aside and reached in to retrieve a book—the book they'd gotten from Bam Rav.

"We'll be needing this," Mara said, before she replaced the stone and lead them to the blacksmith's door.

"What are we doing here?"

In the rarest of moments, Mara actually smiled. "Retrieving your horse."

Saleh.

Amie's heart leapt, and Mara stepped through the doorway and approached the metal master. The man was pointing to an oven, instructing a boy about her age on what he needed to do next. When he sent the boy along, he turned to them, his gaze recognizing Mara after a moment.

"How can I help you, ladies?"

"Earlier," Mara began, "I came here accompanied by two soldiers. We sold you a horse and some other items in exchange for some coin and charcoal. I would like to propose another exchange."

"Is that right?" the blacksmith said. "What do you need?"

"We would like to purchase the horse," Mara said. "In addition, we'd also like fifty gold marks."

The blacksmith stared at the damp pair for a moment before a roar of laughter bellowed from his gut. "And what do you plan to offer in exchange for that? I've already two daughters myself. So the cooking and cleaning is well taken care of."

"Low Lordship," Mara said, "at the very least."

Again, the blacksmith laughed as if Mara were Hzorah's most entertaining bard. "Low Lordship!"

"I noticed that your focus here is nails," Mara said. "I don't suppose there's a smith in the land that doesn't have a steady order for nails, but I also notice that you admire fine weaponry." Mara pointed to the axe mounted on the wall. "Every shop owner needs his defenses, but that axe is no mere axe. You must have saved for weeks for this one. It's fourth-degree Hzorah steel."

The blacksmith's eyes widened with surprise. "You know your axes, girl. I'll give you that."

"You flatter me," Mara said. "But I know steel better than I do weapons themselves."

The blacksmith crossed his arms. "Really?"

"Really," Mara said. "I can teach you how to make fourth-degree Hzorah steel."

Amie joined the blacksmith in slack-jawed disbelief. "What?"

"What?" the blacksmith said in unison with her.

"Not only that," Mara said. "I can teach you how to make it a grade higher than the very axe on your wall once we gather the proper ingredients."

As the blacksmith began to shake his head, Amie jumped in. "She can. You wouldn't believe what she's capable of."

"I don't."

"What do you have to lose?" Amie asked. "At worst, you get to have a laugh and cast us out on our behinds." Amie stepped close. "But if my sister is true to her word, you would have traded several months' pay for a lifetime of fortune."

Pausing to consider her words. The blacksmith rubbed his chin. "Alright. Deal struck."

Mara took his hand but didn't let go. "And if you think to make off with my secrets without the payment I requested, I also know things that will make you curse your mother for daring to bring you into the world of life." Her eyes narrowed. "Is that clear?"

Unsettled, the blacksmith cleared his throat. "Of course. I'm an honest man."

"Good!" Amie said. "I'm glad that's settled. Do you have a pair of boots?"

ADVENTURE AWAITS

Continue your journey for FREE!
Read the next story here:
emergentrealms.com/tcc1

ACKNOWLEDGMENTS

When I first began writing The Continua Chronicles, I always hoped that there would be people who would love the story and characters as much as I did, but I had no idea how humbling it would be when people took the time to let me know how much fun they had with it.

But I'm not doing this alone. It's not just me.

My wife, Pamela, provides me with support and love that helps me continue to write forward. She's also my first reader—the first person I hand the story to when I finish, even before the editor. I couldn't do this without her.

My editor and partner in literary hijinks, Adryanna, was a fantastic help with this story. She makes me sound so much better than I would on my own, and I can't thank her enough for the work she puts into the stories.

Cor S., Megan G., Jean L., Stacie M., Andrew M., Tianna T., and Patrick R. were my beta readers for this project. I appreciate your expedient work and helpful comments.

Finally, I'd like to thank everyone who read and loved the first installment of the series. It's your enthusiasm and positive vibes that encourage me to write stories that fill you with wonder and delight.

ABOUT THE AUTHOR

Jim Wilbourne is a creative at heart. If he's not writing a novel, he's writing and recording a song, or once again trying to learn how to draw. When he's not working on the next project, he spends his free time working on another project. He totally has a life. Jim lives in the deep south with his wife and son and doesn't miss the snow at all.

Lightning Source UK Ltd.
Milton Keynes UK
UKHW022009251022
411088UK00001B/19